CLUES

Down

4. Spin ____ bottle

Across

24. Type of puzzle
35. Inheritance

THE CROSSWORD LEGACY

Herbert Resnicow

Puzzles by Henry Hook

BALLANTINE BOOKS ● NEW YORK

Library of Congress Catalog Card Number: 86-91643

ISBN 0-345-33701-8

Manufactured in the United States of America

First Edition: February 1987

To my son, Norman J., who kept me out of trouble whenever I listened to him.

I am grateful to H. Randolph Williams and to Norman J. Resnicow, both of Baker & McKenzie, for the accurate legal information in this book. Inaccuracies, if any, must be ascribed to my not listening carefully to my expert legal counsel.

"I NEVER HEARD OF A *SECOND* WILL," OLD VICTORIA VAN Broek said peevishly, "and I was present at the reading of Daddy's will." She clamped her mouth shut and sat up stiffly, fixing her eyes on the empty chair behind the big walnut desk.

The six people seated in front of the desk had, without really thinking about it, lined up in order of age. Victoria van Broek, grayer and even more wrinkled than her sixty-six years allowed, was at the far left. Next, though she would have scratched out the eyes of anyone who would have *dared* think the numbers, was forty-nine-year-old Gloria Raffa, her sleek black hair and stylish clothes giving her the look of a woman desperately trying to stay thirty-nine for another few more—just a *few* more—years, God, *please*. On Gloria's right was her cousin Albert Kruger, he of the shaven head and fat neck, chewing an unlit cigar and looking old enough to be Gloria's father, although he was two years younger.

Leading the younger generation, next came Sondra Stempel, whose sour pudgy face, frizzy red hair, and wrinkled clothes hid the brilliant mind that made her, at thirty-three, the most respected, at a distance, mystery editor in New York. After her came the next generation of van Broeks, the great-grandchildren: Richard Deddich, just turned thirty, sat slouched in his chair, his thinning blond hair falling over his pale eyes, the rimless spectacles sliding down his thin nose; and, at the end, little Eileen Ashe, Columbia University school bag between her feet, desperately studying a textbook on contracts.

"Actually, Aunt Victoria"—Albert Kruger cleared his throat noisily—"there can't be a second will. I checked with my lawyer before we came to New York." Francine, Albert's metallic-blond wife, who was sitting on the leather couch against the wall of framed bar certificates and citations, nodded. "Yes," she confirmed, "our lawyer said this can only be part of the first will."

"Then it's all mine," crowed Victoria triumphantly. "I'm the only living child of Cornelius van Broek. I'll have all you leeches thrown out as soon as Mr. Winston comes back." She waved her arthritis-gnarled hand regally at her five blood relations.

"Why are you so anxious to get rid of us, Aunt Vickie?" Gloria Raffa asked. "Because you know you're wrong? Mr. Sullivan sent for us, all of us, not just you. He didn't do it just so we could watch you walk away with everything and leave us with nothing."

"Don't get so excited, Auntie dear," Sondra Stempel said. "At your age, who knows what could happen? Not that it would bother any of us," she added, on second thought, "so go ahead. Start screeching."

"You're a nasty little girl, Sondra," Victoria screeched, pointing a bony finger at the fat young woman, "and you always were. Don't come sniveling to me when you need something."

"Fortunately"—Sondra smiled nastily—"I'll never need anything from you; you're the one who keeps begging me."

"Everybody wonders how a slob like you"—Victoria cackled—"lives so rich on an editor's salary. You couldn't really stand an investigation, Sondra, could you?"

"You sure as hell couldn't, Auntie dear. I have access to all sorts of records."

"You're all against me," Victoria cried. "I'm going to rewrite my will tomorrow. Don't expect a penny, any of you; not one penny."

"We won't, Aunt Vickie," Gloria said. "We know how tight you were, even when you had it."

"My mother used to tell me," Albert Kruger added, "about when we needed a little money, just a little, to save the business, and you turned her down flat. Uncle Jan died of a broken heart when the family lost the business, and you're the one who killed him."

"Jan died of a heart attack," Victoria said, "just like Daddy, because he was a fat pig and smoked those disgusting cigars. You're going to end up exactly the same way, Albert, if you keep on stuffing yourself; it runs in the family. And you better keep a civil tongue in your head if you expect anything from me."

"I don't think any of us are counting on you for anything, Aunt Victoria." He bit his cigar hard. "Not that I need anything from you now, thank God, but we went through some pretty lean years when I was a boy."

"I didn't have anything to give," Victoria said. "It was all invested. Carl and I—."

"Who are you kidding, Vickie?" Gloria Raffa was bitter. "My mother told me the whole story. You had no respect for anything or anyone. You married Carl six months after Grandpa died; couldn't even wait a year for decency."

"We were young, Gloria, in love. Why should we have waited?"

"Love?" Gloria laughed. "You were such a nasty little bitch that only a phony like Carl Locherwald would marry you, and then, only for your money. The two of you were so busy pissing it away that you wouldn't even help your own sisters—"

"They wanted me to"—Victoria's face was white, her mouth drawn back in a snarl. "We each got the same from Daddy; they could have—"

"Jan tried to carry on the business," Albert Kruger said, "and the other three sisters put all their money into it, to carry on the tradition. You didn't."

"My grandmother used to tell me," Eileen Ashe spoke up, "that if you had contributed your share, the business would have survived and flourished. I wouldn't have to fight for scholarships now, and I wouldn't have to work nights."

"My grandmother told me," Richard Deddich said, "that when she came to you, you laughed at her. Laughed. I could have been comptroller of the business by now, instead of . . . and you wouldn't have to live on the insurance income. You did this to all of us. So save your breath, Great-Aunt, I'm not looking to you for anything."

"And don't expect anything from the rest of us either," Gloria Raffa said.

"You ungrateful, unnatural, wretched monsters," Victoria cursed. "You, and Albert, too, have been doing well, so very well, for years, and you know how tiny my income is. These days, I can hardly afford to eat, but do you . . . ? Whenever I write, you don't even answer me. And you expect me to

3

give you something, anything, from my inheritance? I'd rather burn it than—"

"You try anything like that, Auntie," Gloria said heavily, "and you'll regret it. But *really* regret it. There are things my mother told me about you, Auntie, that you wouldn't want to have known. So you be careful what you do, especially if it involves me. And watch what you say, too."

"Your past isn't so perfect either, Gloria," Victoria said viciously. "What I could tell about you could make some very big trouble for you, too. So don't you threaten me, Gloria. I'm sure your clients would just love to know about the deals you make behind their backs."

"Stop this," Albert shouted. "Are you two crazy? We don't know what the will says. Don't start making trouble over guesswork; you could hurt all our chances. And remember this: anything we have to say about the family, we say *inside* the family, right? Not in front of outsiders. Ever. Got it?"

"Don't you yell at me, you nasty fat pig," Victoria replied. "There are plenty of stories about how you got your first store that might still get you in trouble today."

"You try pulling any stuff like that, Aunt Victoria," Albert said vehemently, "and you'll have some real serious problems. Part of that inheritance is mine, and you better not do anything to spoil the deal."

"What are you so worried about, Uncle Albert?" Eileen asked. "You're rich; you don't need any more money. I'm the one who's really broke here."

"You can always use more money," Albert said. "Anybody can. But I'm not greedy. All I want is my share. My *fair* share. And I'll do what I have to do to make sure I get it. Is that clear?" He looked at each of the others in turn.

"We'll all do," Richard Deddich said, "whatever we have to do to get our fair share. But who decides what's fair, Uncle Albert? You?"

"When the will is read ... The way I see it," Albert said, "we six are the only living direct descendants of Cornelius van Broek, and we've been called here for the reading of the will which, my lawyer said, has to be part of the original will that was read here forty-three years ago. Under that will, Aunt Victoria got hers already, so she doesn't get a second dip from the barrel." The old lady started to get up, but Gloria pushed her back, not too gently. "I'm not finished yet, Aunt Victoria; you can talk later. So I figure we each get one-fifth, at least. Or if it was done right, Gloria, Susan, and I, as Cornelius's grandchildren, get two shares each, since we have twice as much van Broek blood as the great-grandchildren, and Richard and Eileen get one share each. So Gloria, Susan, and I get a quarter of the inheritance each, and these two get an eighth each."

"Now that you've made all the arrangements, Uncle Albert," Richard Deddich said sarcastically, "why bother reading the will? We'll just sign over our shares to you and go home."

"Are you sure we're the only direct descendants?" Eileen asked. "I haven't really had the time to keep up with the family history. Isn't it possible that ... ?"

"Not a chance," Gloria said. "Mr. Sullivan must have spent the last year checking to see if there were any possible illegitimate claimants. I'm sure we're the only ones."

"Don't start looking for complications, Eileen," Sondra Stempel said, "and don't start asking Mr. Sullivan any stupid questions. The fewer of us there are, the more each one of us gets."

"GOOD NEWS, SIR," OLIVER SAID AS HE RETURNED. "MISS Macintosh's plane is due in half an hour."

"And it will be stacked up for another fifteen minutes," Giles Sullivan said ruefully. "Did you call Henry Winston?"

"Yes, sir. He says the natives are getting restless and urges you to come to the office at once."

"There's nothing like the smell of money, Oliver, to drive perfectly normal people crazy. Did you explain to Henry that I had to pick up Isabel?"

"I was certain he would not understand, sir, how upset Miss Macintosh would be if you were not here to greet her. And I am afraid, sir, she will consider the plane's delay as your personal responsibility, which will set back your campaign to get her to give up driving her surplus jeep here from Vermont."

"That jeep is old, decrepit, and dangerous, Oliver, and even with the normal airline delays, she will get here hours sooner than if she had driven."

"Quite true, sir, but Miss Macintosh is prone to overlook such mundane details when in the grip of righteous indignation at your minor delinquencies, particularly if the events in question are not under your direct control."

"I don't suppose," Giles asked apprehensively, "that this airline provides chocolates for its passengers?"

"Not even American chocolate bars, sir, which have cereals displacing the essential anodyne."

"You did bring... ?"

"Certainly, sir. Dutch, this time. I have no wish to be described by the lady as an epicure manqué. At length."

"And the minute she opens her mouth, you will pop in a piece—make that two pieces—of—"

"I'm afraid not, sir. All I could get on such short notice

was a Droste Apple which, after unwrapping, must be tapped on a hard surface to separate itself into segments. This will take several seconds, sir, during which Miss Macintosh will have shifted into high gear and become, for an extended period of time, unstoppable."

"It's all her fault, Oliver. She wasn't supposed to be here for another week."

"Quite so, sir, but I am afraid it will count for naught. She will, rightly, expect you to be overjoyed that she could visit you all the sooner."

"I am, Oliver, of course I am. But she couldn't have come at a worse time, what with the reading of the van Broek will and all."

"The reading of the will, sir, is a relatively minor matter, a one-Droste-Apple problem, compared to—"

"You got only *one* Apple, Oliver?"

"It was all that store had left, sir. She called from the airport at the last minute and, as it was, had her plane been on time, we would have been several minutes late."

"Oliver, she can finish one Apple before we get out of the parking lot. Are you fully prepared at home?"

"I had ordered a sufficient supply of chocolates, cocoa, and syrup, sir, all Dutch, for next week. After we get back, I shall scour the stores and we will be completely restocked in short order."

"Which could take you hours, Oliver. When we get home, she'll find out the truth."

"I had thought of that sir, and I suggest that, instead of going home first, you take Miss Macintosh to Mr. Winston's office and have her sit through the reading of Mr. van Broek's will."

"She really has no business being at the reading, Oliver. It's highly irregular."

"If Miss Macintosh were required to wait in the reception room, she would be most unhappy. I am sure, sir, you could provide some reason to involve the lady in the reading. That will give me an opportunity to purchase a temporarily appeasing stock of Swiss chocolates, and Miss Macintosh will learn the awful truth gradually."

"Which will make her all the more furious afterward, Oliver. She will think I deliberately fooled her. Did you consider that?"

"True, sir, but Miss Macintosh is too much of a lady to express herself fully in front of strangers."

"But when we get home, Oliver?"

"I will make sure that some of the new help will always be around, so that you will be spared—"

"But when we're alone in my bedroom...?"

"Let us hope, sir, that by then, Miss Isabel's passions will have subsided."

Giles glared at his butler. "You have a very odd way, Oliver, of wishing me well."

"American is not my native tongue, sir," Oliver said blandly. "One more thing, sir. I shall need a hard surface on which to tap the Droste Apple. The big gold head of your cane, perhaps? If you will just hand it to me, sir?"

"So you can *accidentally* trip and break the cane as you fall?" Giles moved the cane to the side away from Oliver. "Never, Oliver. I fear I may need it today."

"You would *stab* Miss Macintosh, sir?"

"Don't be silly, Oliver. Only as a shield."

"Your cane might be effective against another saber, sir, but against a rapier tongue...? Possibly earmuffs?"

"Isabel would take that as a personal insult, Oliver."

"Possibly we could turn Miss Macintosh's unexpected arrival into an opportunity to revise the arrangements you have made for the accommodation of the van Broek heirs?"

"Totally unnecessary, Oliver; the situation is ideal. I spent a month planning every detail."

"We have had situations in the past, sir, when well-planned actions had to be changed at the last moment due to unforeseen circumstances. Usually with disastrous results."

"We are not dealing with that sort of person here, Oliver. The van Broek heirs are all sound, stable people; honest, respectable citizens. Dependable. I had them investigated thoroughly."

"Yes, sir, but only in their usual habitat. Under the conditions you propose, sir..."

"I don't want to hear any more about it, Oliver; we will continue as I had originally planned. If you have taken care of your part of the assignment properly, in accordance with my instructions, there cannot be the slightest problem."

"If you say so, sir."

Henry Winston was barely seated behind his big walnut desk when Victoria van Broek pinned him with her sharp blue eyes. "It's ten-thirty already," she complained. "Mr. Sullivan told us to be here at ten sharp. A person could die of old age waiting."

"Now that she's brought it up," Sondra Stempel said, smiling at the thought, "what happens if Aunt Victoria dies before the will is read?"

"You greedy little harpy"—Victoria bared her teeth—"counting my money already?"

"Please, ladies," Henry Winston begged, "this is not the time and place. Possibly you have some general questions? Until Mr. Sullivan arrives?"

"Is this a different will," Victoria asked, "or the same will that was read when Daddy passed away?"

"It's part of the same will, Miss van Broek. If there were a later will, it would have been read then."

"Then it's all mine," Victoria crowed triumphantly. "I'm the only living child of Cornelius van Broek. None of these ghouls"—she waved her hand at the other five—"was even alive when the will was written, so they couldn't have been in it."

"It's not quite like that," Winston said cautiously. "Your father's will, after providing for the family, servants, and employees, made sizable charitable bequests and established a trust."

"Daddy left as much to that trust as he did to me," Victoria snapped. "We assumed it was another of his charities; that he had directed the bank's trust department to pass out *our* money to a bunch of lazy loafers."

"Actually," Winston said dryly, "it was to be invested and be passed out to . . . That's why you six are here."

9

"When I was told that this was to be about a possible inheritance from my great-grandfather," Richard said quietly, "I spoke to a fellow in my office, an expert in annuities. He said you can't have a will that's effective fifty years after a testator's death. It's called a will in perpetuity."

"If you have an alternate heir, Mr. Deddich, preferably a nonprofit organization which is likely to have a life beyond the provisions of the will, you can make a will to take effect for an even longer period. The idea is that, if there are none of the named heirs extant at that time, the institution will be there to accept the inheritance."

"You mean Daddy left even *more* money to that damned Cruciverbal Club?" Victoria shrilled. "In addition to my house? There was no way to know that the club would exist this long."

"Your father left *his* mansion to the club," Winston said patiently, "with possession only upon the death of your mother. The Cruciverbal Club would have been an unsuitable alternate heir; the Boy Scouts of America was chosen. Since you six are here, they have no interest in this will."

"You seem to know all about the will, Mr. Winston," Sondra said. "Why don't you read it to us?"

"I'm here, Miss Stempel, because Mr. Sullivan has been delayed. He is the one who must read the will."

"I'm still concerned," Richard said stubbornly, "about the validity of this will. Suppose Eileen and I, as the only great-grandchildren, get the major part of the inheritance. I can just see Aunt Gloria, and Sondra and Albert, too, running to their lawyers and tying up the estate for years. And what if everything were left to Great-Aunt Victoria? She's the only one who carries the van Broek name now. Would that be legal? She's already inherited once under this very same will."

"It's not my fault, Richard"—Victoria showed her false teeth in a cold smile—"that your grandmother lost everything in business. I have a perfect right to my own Daddy's money."

"You'd be the first to scream, dear nephew"—Gloria Raffa patted her too-black hair with crimson-tipped hands—"if you didn't get more than your share. Don't project your fantasies on me, kid."

"I need that money worse than you do, Richard"—Sondra

Stempel glared at the pale young man—"and I have twice as many van Broek genes as you do."

"All I want is what's coming to me"—Kruger shifted his heavy body clumsily in the chair—"and I'm going to get it, one way or another."

"Please, please, ladies, gentlemen." Henry Winston made smoothing motions with his hands. "Mr. Sullivan worked with several of our senior partners in the past year and even consulted an outside specialist, H. Randolph Williams of Baker & McKenzie, a recognized expert on wills and estates. This will was drawn by my grandfather, a highly respected legal scholar. There is no doubt in anyone's mind that the legal provisions of the will are perfectly in order."

"I sincerely hope so"—Eileen Ashe smiled sweetly—"because I need the money to get my doctorate and I don't want any problems. I have some boyfriends in Columbia Law School who would be happy to research the case for me, if I felt I was not being treated fairly. Some professors, too."

"I think I'd better go and see where Mr. Sullivan is." Henry Winston slipped quietly out of the office and shut the door firmly behind him.

Albert Kruger watched the door. As soon as it was shut, he turned to Eileen Ashe. "The trouble with you, Eileen"—Kruger grinned around his cigar—"is that you're young. Which means ignorant. Not necessarily stupid"—he waved her objection aside—"just that you haven't lived long enough to learn some things. My lawyer once told me that the worst settlement is better than the best lawsuit. Usually. You're threatening that if you don't get what you want, you and your bunch of amateurs and longhair professors are going to tie up the estate? Well, you can probably do that. I have lawyers, too, and I have money. So does Gloria. I'm sure that Sondra can also find a lawyer or two. Richard has plenty of lawyers at the insurance company where he works. So we'll have five sets of lawyers fighting each other. Maybe even six. Aunt Victoria will get a lawyer, too; she's got a good case. Six sets of lawyers. You know what that means, Eileen? *Bleak House*, that's what it means. The legal costs will eat up the estate, the whole estate, and we, the heirs, will get nothing. Zero. None of us."

"Albert didn't mention the worst thing," Gloria added.

"You'll also be fighting the estate. Giles Sullivan and all of Winston and Harrigan. They don't have to worry about money; anything they spend comes out of the estate. The more you attack, the more money they make. It's like fighting the IRS. They're using *your* money, *our* money, to fight *us*. Forget about a lawsuit, Eileen; that kills everybody's chances."

"There's got to be something I can do," Eileen said, "to make sure I get—"

"Oh, there is." Richard Deddich smiled wickedly. "In the insurance business, we come across many instances of it. Ask Aunt Sondra; she's an expert."

"Whodunits? They're fiction, Richard, and I don't plot them; I only edit them. So don't start setting me up as patsy for whatever *you're* planning behind that baby face."

"How quickly"—Gloria shook her head sadly—"how easily, this younger generation slides into—into easy answers. That's your *only* solution, Richard? Cut down the competition? There's no other way we can all win? Well let me tell you"—her voice grew hard—"let me *warn* you, in thirty years in the flesh-peddling business I've had plenty of experience with this kind of crap, and I'm still here. You, any of you, *start* anything with me, *anything*, and I'll finish it." Her glare swept the five faces in turn.

"**O**LIVER! STOP!" ISABEL MACINTOSH SNAPPED HER HEAD around. "You drove past the—"

"We have to drop in at the office for a moment," Giles said smoothly.

"*The* office?" Isabel grated. "*Henry Winston's* office? The one you *retired* from? Instead of taking me home? After you haven't seen me for two months?"

"Yes, well, the, uh, appointment was made a month ago."

"Cary Grant would have considered the world well lost for the woman he loved. Abelard—"

"But you called just this morning," Giles protested. "From the airport. You were supposed to come *next* Wednesday."

"I had a sudden desire to see you, Sullivan, fool that I was. So I dropped everything, cancelled *my* appointments, *all* my appointments, and made a mad dash to the airport. *Raced* to the airport, Sullivan; risked my *life*. To wait on *standby*. Which I got *moments* before the takeoff, barely time to call you. And you have *an* appointment? Hah!"

"It's— There are six people waiting, Isabel, all the preparations and everything. Please."

"*Six* people, Sullivan? Well, now I know how I stand with you. That's really flattering, Sullivan, that it takes an appointment with *six* people to outweigh your mad desire to be alone with me. Where's the dividing line, Sullivan; five people? Would you stand up *five* people for me? How about four adults and a child? Three and a dog? A *big* dog? *One?* What *am* I worth to you, Sullivan? How many clients equal one Isabel Macintosh? Next you're going to tell me there are millions involved, right, Sullivan?"

"As a matter of fact, yes, there are. But they—these six— aren't clients, Isabel; not really. Actually, there's only one client, and he's dead, but—"

"One *dead* client, Sullivan? And *he* takes precedence over me? That does it, Sullivan. You've done some pretty rotten things in your day, Sullivan, but this takes the cake. One dead client is more important to you than I am?"

"But, Isabel, it isn't like that at all. The appointment was made—that is, the date was selected fifty years ago—so I can't—"

"Fifty *years* ago? And you're in such a hurry you can't go home with me for an hour or two first? After being apart for two whole months? And my almost being killed in Washington? Midsummer in Washington? Where it's *hot*? Too hot to even—"

"It's *because* the date was set fifty years ago that— Look, Isabel, I really am glad to—that is, extremely happy, *overjoyed* that you're here. While I was waiting I figured out how you could fit into the arrangement so that we—"

"You can *use* me in your *business*, is that it? Be still, my fluttering heart; was there ever so romantic a proposal since love began? Surely this declamation will set new standards for passion, new pinnacles for star-struck lovers to climb, new—"

"But I really—"

"Oh, shut up, Sullivan; you're digging your grave deeper and deeper every time you open your mouth. One of these days, Sullivan, you'll *begin* to learn how to *start* to understand how to—"

"Here we are, Miss Macintosh," Oliver announced. "Do you want to stay with me while I park?"

"Park? Sullivan, you said it was just for a—How long is this moment you mentioned, Sullivan? In real time, I mean?"

"Well, uh, I just read a little and explain a little and answer a few questions a little, then we all go home."

"I'm going up there with you, Sullivan. To clock you."

"Yes. Of course. Excellent idea. That way you can meet— Yes. Fine. We'll go up together. Ha! Yes. Perfect."

"I get very suspicious, Sullivan, when you start dithering. Oliver, before you park, get me some chocolate. It may very well save your master's life. Lots of chocolate. One Droste Apple is not enough. The quotation, you may remember, is '...comfort me with apples...' *Apples*, Oliver, not *apple*. Plural. Lots of them. Got it?"

Oliver closed the car door, locked it, then carefully opened

14

the window exactly one inch. "I will get you a *case* of Droste Apples, Miss Isabel; I hope it will be enough for your needs. I *do* remember the quotation, Miss Isabel; it is from the Song of Songs: '. . . comfort me with apples: for I am sick of love.'" He quickly rolled up the window and sped off.

"I APOLOGIZE FOR MY LATENESS," GILES SULLIVAN SAID as he sat down behind Henry Winston's desk. "Miss Macintosh's plane was delayed." Isabel looked at him without expression from the couch against the wall.

"What does she have to do," Sondra Stempel asked suspiciously, "with the reading of the will?"

"Not with the reading as such," Giles answered, "but she will have an important function later, in the implementation of . . ." He carefully avoided Isabel's eyes. "Let me introduce Isabel Macintosh, acting president of Windham University, who has ably assisted me in several, uh, legal matters. And you must be Sondra Stempel, granddaughter of Cornelius van Broek and a topnotch mystery editor. I'm a great mystery fan myself and my man, Oliver, is an avid collector of whodunits."

"Good," Sondra said. "I need all the sales I can get."

"This would be a good opportunity for you all to be introduced to Miss Macintosh, since in the next few days"—a hiss of indrawn breath was heard from the couch—"you will have, uh—some contact with the lady. I, myself, have spent so much time, uh, preparing for this day that I feel I know you all intimately."

"You've had us investigated?" Albert Kruger looked wary.

"Only to insure that you were, indeed, the only living direct descendants of Cornelius van Broek. And you are, of course, grandson Albert Kruger, who holds soft–ice-cream franchises in Oswego. And the lady next to Miss Macintosh on the couch must be your wife, Francine."

"You should have let us know you were investigating," Kruger said. "If you're trying to get a business loan, somebody checking up on you can turn off a bank very fast."

"It was all done very discreetly, I assure you, Mr. Kruger.

Going to your left is Gloria Raffa, granddaughter, who is the best-known theatrical agent in New York. Next to her is Miss Victoria van Broek, daughter of Cornelius, who is retired."

"That's very genteel, Mr. Sullivan," Victoria said bitterly. "Living in poverty because her rich relatives are too cheap to help out their aunt, might be a better way to put it."

"Yes, well, Miss Victoria, possibly after I read the will, you will take heart. Your father often told me how clever his youngest daughter was at—at so many things."

"Nonsense, Mr. Sullivan; he hated me."

"No, no, Miss Victoria. He admired you very much; you were so like him in so many ways. Your father only disapproved of—certain headstrong tendencies of yours. But let's pass on to Richard Deddich, great-grandson, who is an actuary for a health-insurance company, and to Miss Eileen Ashe, great-granddaughter, a graduate student, law, at Columbia University."

Each turned to nod at Isabel and murmur a few polite words. Isabel held her lips in a professional greeter's tight smile and nodded in turn, as though not trusting her ability to control her speech.

"Let's get back to business," Kruger said. "I asked Winston some questions before, and I didn't get complete answers. Is this will a perpetual will or is it legal? And tell me in plain English."

"This will is a legal instrument, in force as of this date. If you will permit me to go through the formal reading, I am sure all your questions will be answered fully."

"I don't need every 'whereas' and 'wherefore' read to me," Gloria said. "Just the important parts. Then give me a certified copy of the whole will to take with me."

"If that's agreeable to the rest of you ... ?" Giles's eyes went around the room. "No objections?" He waited.

"Get on with it, Mr. Sullivan," Victoria said impatiently.

"Very well, then." Giles's voice shifted to formal. "Cornelius van Broek was a great gentleman. I knew him in his last years before the unfortunate attack that took him in his prime. Through our mutual interest in word games, which led to the founding of the Cruciverbal Club, I got to know him quite well."

"Were you the one," Victoria broke in, "who tricked him

into giving my house to that club?"

"No, Miss Victoria. I didn't know his intentions until the will was read, and I did not become executor of the estate until some years later. But let me continue. Cornelius van Broek believed in, and lived, the Ten Commandments. He was a patriot in the very best sense of the word, and an active and generous supporter of the Boy Scouts, as well as of many other charities. One of his concerns, more fully expressed in the handwritten instructions he gave Arnold Winston for the formalization of his will, was that his direct descendants, you ladies and gentlemen, should not have to go through the same hardships he faced when he came here as a penniless young boy."

There was a great sigh around the room. "I knew it," Victoria said. "Daddy would never let me down."

"Cornelius van Broek was well aware of the saying, 'shirt-sleeves to shirt-sleeves in three generations.' He was deter-mined that, no matter how profligate his children were, his grandchildren and great-grandchildren, those with his blood in their veins—now we would say, 'those who inherited his genes'—would have a chance, a door opened for them, which would allow them to make of themselves that which their van Broek genes permitted."

"How big is the estate?" Gloria asked huskily.

"Your grandfather left ten percent of his liquid assets in control of the trust department of his bank, with instructions to invest for whoever would inherit it on the hundredth anni-versary of Cornelius van Broek's birth."

"You lawyers are all alike," Sondra sneered. "How much, Mr. Sullivan? In round numbers."

"In round numbers, Miss Stempel, about eighteen million dollars."

They all smiled, relieved. "Good," said Kruger. "Three million each. Just right."

"No," Giles said, "I'm sorry. It isn't."

"Taxes, Mr. Sullivan?" Victoria asked. "I am quite pre-pared to pay my share to the tax collector. What is left is quite enough for my needs."

"What I meant was . . . that's the trouble with shortcuts; I should have just read the will. Mr. van Broek bequeathed the entire amount to that one, and only one, of his direct descendants who best exemplified the van Broek characteristics as he saw them, and the ideals he lived by."

"The Ten Commandments?" Eileen said. "That's easy. I'm too young to have sinned as much as Uncle Albert and Aunt Gloria. Even Richard is almost ten years older than I am. That's ten years of sin, Mr. Sullivan. If he's like all my other relatives."

"Not just the Ten Commandments, Miss Ashe. The Boy Scout laws and the American ideal, as expressed by the Declaration of Independence and the Constitution. He had a great admiration for these expressions of ethics and free-dom. More important, he wanted to reward what he saw as his own personal characteristics: intelligence, tenacity, patience, hard work, fortitude, honesty, respect for law, good business sense, the ability to solve problems under pressure and—I'm sure this comes from his deep interest in cross-words—facility with words."

"Well, I have all of that," Gloria Raffa said. "I've fought my way to the top in the toughest profession in New York. Some of the creeps I represent are as hard to deal with and to keep out of jail as the producers on the other side of the table. There is no harder job in the world."

"I'm a senior editor," Sondra Stempel said, "in a business where the average tenure is measured in months. I've had four bestsellers in the past three years. They bet millions on my judgment."

"I'm the only one here who's ever met a real payroll and paid, on time, big business loans." Albert Kruger leaned back in his chair confidently. "I put my money where my mouth is. As far as words are concerned, anyone who can convince a loan officer to extend a million-dollar line of credit to a guy who is practically bankrupt—well, just try it your-self."

"No, no," Giles silenced them. "I'm sure everybody believes that he alone deserves to be the heir. But Mr. van Broek foresaw that. He set up an objective test, a set of tests, designed to show who most closely resembles his ideal heir, who deserves to inherit the money."

"Are you saying, Mr. Sullivan"—Victoria's voice trem-bled—"that only one of us can inherit my own Daddy's money? That I may get nothing?"

"I'm sorry, Miss Victoria, but whoever passes the tests first wins all. But in the event there is no clear winner, which is most unlikely, I am empowered to apply further tests."

"You, Mr. Sullivan?" Richard asked. "You have the power to decide if I am more like my great-grandfather than, say, Eileen?"

"I won't make the decision subjectively. I would use more tests of the same nature as the first set, but somewhat more difficult. Whoever passed those tests first, would win."

"Suppose I don't want to take the tests?" Kruger said. "Suppose I just sue to set those provisions aside?"

"Then, by the provisions of the will, you cut yourself out of any consideration at all. Before you think of suing, I suggest you talk to your attorney."

"What if I take the tests," Kruger went on, "don't win, and then sue?"

"That was foreseen, too, Mr. Kruger. In order to take the tests, you must first sign an agreement to accept the test results and give up all rights to litigation involving the will and the tests. As an old litigator, Mr. Kruger, I again advise you to take the tests. From my knowledge of you, you have an excellent chance of winning. You're a mature, successful business man, educated, intelligent, and a prime example, in many ways, of the van Broek ideal."

"Are you prejudiced in Albert's favor, Mr. Sullivan?" Sondra asked. "Because if you are . . ."

"Not at all, Miss Stempel. I am totally disinterested. If I have any interest at all, it is that van Broek's wishes come true: that the winner shows the van Broek characteristics to a high degree."

"Before I even consider signing up, Sullivan," Kruger said, "what are the tests like?"

"I'll *read* this part, to make sure there is no misunderstanding." Giles picked up the will. "'. . . a series of crossword puzzles which, when solved, will provide the message which leads to the inheritance. When you have all the words written down, the key will appear.' That's it, in its entirety."

"Crosswords, eh?" Kruger smiled wolfishly. "I don't think I'll sue, after all. Where do I sign?"

Isabel Macintosh walked to behind Giles's chair and held her left wrist in front of his face, her watch directly opposite his eyes. "How long is a moment, Sullivan?" she whispered in his ear.

"We're almost finished," he whispered back. "Sit down,

and for God's sake, don't make a fuss about—about anything."

"About what, Sullivan?" She took her hand down. "Are
you delicately hinting that it's going to get worse? What could
be worse than what you've already done?"

"Not *worse*, Isabel. Just—different. A *little* different.
You'll find it very—very interesting. Yes. Very. Now please
sit down; you're being conspicuous."

"**Y**OU MEAN," VICTORIA ASKED, "THAT WHOEVER SOLVES Daddy's crossword puzzles wins *everything*? That's wonderful. Daddy taught me himself; I know how he thinks."

"Crosswords?" Gloria glowed. "Hell, I do them in ink while I'm negotiating with the sharpest producers in New York."

"I do free-lance copyediting for extra money," Sondra said. "Nobody has a greater knowledge of words than an editor. Or of trivia."

"That's really unfair." Eileen's face was red. "I'm very good at crosswords, but I can see that everyone else has been doing them years longer than I have. Even Richard. Look at him. He isn't saying a word, but he looks like the cat that swallowed the canary. You can't put me at such a disadvantage, Mr. Sullivan. I'm sure that wasn't my great-grandfather's intent."

"I can't change the rules, Miss Ashe. It's not how fast you solve the crosswords that's important; I know van Broek's constructions, and he wasn't that great a constructor. I suspect the solving of the crosswords will be relatively easy, probably no harder than a Friday *Times* puzzle of today. It's the message, which is evidently concealed in the puzzles, that will really test your capabilities."

"How much time will we have?" Richard asked.

"To solve the puzzles? A day each."

"So solving the puzzles a few minutes faster won't be important?"

"It will give you that much more time, Mr. Deddich, to analyze, to find the message. And when you do, a five-minute lead may be important."

"How many puzzles are there?"

"Three. At least to begin with."

"And we have a whole day for each? Are they fair puzzles? Honest clues? Real words?"

"I don't think Mr. van Broek would make it impossible to solve the crosswords. He *did* want one of you to win. But I am sure there will be some degree of difficulty in finding the hidden message, the key to the inheritance. For that, you may very well need the full three days."

"What happens," Sondra asked, "if more than one of us finds the key?"

"Whoever is first, Miss Stempel, to find the message, becomes the sole heir. But there is a time limit for the tests. The contest will end in exactly one week; at twelve noon, next Wednesday."

"A *week*?" Isabel couldn't help it.

"I have every hope, Miss Macintosh," Giles said, "that the contest will be over in less time than that. Mr. van Broek had a somewhat straightforward way of thinking. I doubt that his message will be so well hidden, or so complex, that any of you cannot ferret it out in a relatively short time."

"What happens," Kruger asked, "if no one solves the problem by that time?"

"If no one has won by the day after you get the last of the three puzzles, I will give you all one or more additional tests designed to determine which of you has the greatest proportion of the desired qualities in his makeup. Or hers."

"Suppose," Kruger said thoughtfully, "what I said before. About dividing up the inheritance equally. You said it was to go to only one person. Okay, but what if we all work together; designate one person to be the winner, sign papers that he shares equally with all of us, and we all cooperate. We're more likely to find the answer that way and we'd each get enough money to satisfy our needs."

"Even if that were allowed, only one person is permitted to inherit. The will specifies the *one* person who most clearly exhibits the characteristics Cornelius specified, as measured by the test. If I saw any evidence of collaboration, I would disqualify both you and your associate at once."

"You would be judge, jury, and executioner, Mr. Sullivan?" Victoria asked.

"In such matters, yes. The papers you sign before the tests are passed out provide that you accept my decision as final and binding."

23

"Who judges if I've won?" Sondra asked. "*When* I've won, I mean."

"There was no provision for such judgment in the will, Miss Stempel, so the presumption must be that winning will be self-evident: some action or achievement that will be visible to everyone."

"Will we be allowed references, Mr. Sullivan?" Eileen asked.

"Oh, yes, Miss Ashe, I—. There will be available to you a very large selection of crossword dictionaries, encyclopedias, and reference books of all kinds. You will also have available to you, as a consultant, in case any problem arises out of the crosswords themselves, one of the greatest crossword experts in New York, Mrs. Lila Quinn, Chairman of the Board of the New York Cruciverbal Club. She will also function as judge of the contest, to avoid any claim of bias on my part."

"What is there to judge?" Eileen asked. "If the winning will be self-evident, who needs a judge?"

"There may be some dispute as to whether or not the presumed action or achievement was indeed the correct one. There may be some question as to whether or not the claimed winner does indeed exhibit the characteristics Cornelius van Broek admired. Oh, yes, there must be a judge, an impartial judge, for your protection as well as for mine."

"Who the hell is this Mrs. Quinn," Gloria asked, "to decide if I win or not? What makes you so sure she's impartial? Or honest? What right do you have to anoint her judge?"

"I have every right to do so, Miss Raffa, as executor of the will, and Mrs. Quinn is, I feel, the person best qualified for that function. She is unquestionably the best crossword solver in the New York area, and a person of the highest integrity. If you question that, I suggest you try to bribe her for whatever good you think it will do you. You will find yourself disqualified before you draw another breath. Mrs. Quinn is also a person who gets things done fast and well. When the chairmanship of the board of directors of the Cruciverbal Club fell vacant last fall, Mrs. Quinn was unanimously chosen to fill that position by the other directors, people who had worked with her for three years or more."

"What is this Cruciverbal Club?" Albert Kruger asked. "I've been doing crosswords all my life and I've never heard of it."

"That may be because you live so far from New York City," Giles explained, "and our publicity committee may need a touch of Lila Quinn's sharp tongue. We're quite well known to the crossword professionals and to the local crossword and word game fans. The club was founded a little over fifty years ago by a small group of people who loved word puzzles, and especially crosswords, Cornelius van Broek among them. They wanted to promote word puzzles and games, to have a place where people of similar interests could meet and exchange views, to hold annual contests for solving and constructing puzzles, and to encourage and patronize the study of words and language. The Club is now housed in what was once the van Broek mansion, a short distance south of this office on Fifth Avenue. I am attorney for the club and Miss Macintosh is a respected member. So you see, in order to avoid my being judge, jury and executioner, as Miss Victoria pointed out, I will be the referee, and leave the judging in the very able hands of Mrs. Quinn."

"Is that what Miss Macintosh will do too?" Richard asked.

"Precisely." Giles smiled quickly at Isabel. She smiled back, but it was a different kind of smile. "And she will assist in—uh, other administrative duties."

"What exactly will Mrs. Quinn and Miss Macintosh do for us?" Richard asked.

"Clarify ambivalent matters, get you the reference books you request, suggest reference sources, and, if you wish, give you *general* tips on advanced crossword solving."

"So we can get outside help," Kruger said, "but we can't collaborate? Sounds stupid."

"No, you most definitely *cannot* get outside help; you must solve the puzzles *yourself*, and you must find the hidden message *yourself*. Mrs. Quinn and Miss Macintosh will grease the gears, so to speak, not do your work for you."

"You're going to stop me from talking to my wife, Mr. Sullivan?" Kruger asked. "Fat chance."

"Well, yes, Mr. Kruger, I must do exactly that. The will specifies that we are looking for the individual who solves the puzzles and finds the message, not who has the smartest wife."

"Jail, Mr. Sullivan? Solitary confinement?"

"Well, no, Mr. Kruger. Not exactly. When I found there were six of you, I immediately realized that—"

"You didn't, Sullivan!" Isabel was on her feet. "Of all the dirty—"

"Please, Miss Macintosh," Giles said sternly. "You are upsetting our guests. We will discuss this at the appropriate time and place." Isabel sat down, stiffly. Giles turned back to Kruger. "I was concerned that there would be no way to control the, uh, efforts by some of you to make use of outside, uh, consultants. With eighteen million at stake, it would be easy to retain experts in cryptography and such other skills as to enable one of you to find the hidden message in contravention of the provisions of the will. When it turned out that there were six of you, that problem solved itself."

"Six is the magic number?" Eileen asked.

"I have a large brownstone, Miss Ashe, in which I have lived alone for the past eighteen years. The third and fourth floors, which have three bedrooms each, have been shut off."

"We're going to live in *your* house?" Sondra asked.

"You'll be very comfortable. Ping is an excellent cook and Oliver the perfect butler. You will be treated as guests in a luxurious home; nothing but the best at your disposal."

"So how will you keep my wife from talking to me?" Kruger asked. "Hidden cameras? Bug my room?"

"That would be an invasion of your privacy as my guest, Mr. Kruger. No, your wife may remain at her present hotel; the estate will pay all costs."

Francine got up from the couch, smiling. "Don't worry about me, Albert; go ahead and win the eighteen million. You'll need it. I'm going to go shopping for a *week*." She walked out of the office. Kruger watched her go without moving a muscle.

"Do you mean we go *now*?" Eileen asked. "Right now? What about my books? Clothes? Makeup? Everything?"

"I have manuscripts to read," Sondra protested, "and to edit."

"I need my special pen," Victoria said. "I can't hold a thin one. And thick-handled silver. Toothbrush. Lots of things."

"We have chauffeured limousines waiting downstairs, which will drive you to your homes, and you to your hotel, Mr. Kruger. The chauffeurs will also help you pack, but don't bother taking too much; everything you need will be provided. If you have to be driven to your place of business, for any reason, or your school, Miss Ashe, that will be done, too. But whatever you do, you must do quickly. You will be expected to be at my home two hours after this meeting ends. Once you're settled, and you find you've forgotten some necessity, don't worry; it will be provided. You can keep whatever you've been given."

"What's the hurry?" Gloria asked. "I have a business to run, two very important deals cooking. Why don't we just make our preparations today and meet at your house tomorrow?"

"Two reasons, Miss Raffa. First, the will specified that the contest would start on the hundredth anniversary of Cornelius van Broek's birth, and I intend to follow the instructions to the letter. I don't want any claims later that I did not carry out my brief properly."

"And the second reason?" Richard asked.

"Please don't any of you take this personally, but I didn't want any of you to be able to make arrangements to communicate with outside consultants once you're in my house."

"The chauffeur will follow me around?" Sondra was outraged.

"He will not infringe on your personal privacy, Miss Stempel, but he will be next to you whenever you communicate with anyone in any way."

"I suppose the estate pays for all this?" Kruger asked sarcastically.

"It does, Mr. Kruger, but I think if you analyze the situation, my solution will cost the estate far less than if we took over one floor of a small hotel, with much worse security. I am charging no rent, only the direct additional costs."

"I wouldn't mind living in a mansion again," Victoria said dreamily. "It would be fitting. But I have a problem, Mr. Sullivan. I can't write fast; I have to use a special pen. My fingers—" She held out a pair of knobby hands. "I've developed some arthritis and I have to move more slowly. You should give me my puzzles an hour before you give the others theirs."

"If you do that," Sondra said, "you should penalize her for being trained by her father, who made the test puzzles."

"I'm sorry, Miss Victoria," Giles said. "I can't give anyone preference. Now, if there are no more questions, Miss

Macintosh and I will escort you downstairs."

Giles stood up. Isabel took him by the arm lovingly and whispered in his ear. "You have really outdone yourself this time, Sullivan. That was the lowest thing I can even *conceive* of your doing. Guess where *you're* going to sleep tonight?"

"I can't," he whispered. "Lila Quinn will be in the second-floor guest bedroom."

"On top of everything, I won't even have privacy on my own floor? Even there? I'll get you for this, Sullivan."

"Yes," Giles said wearily. "I know. But later."

"Count on it, Sullivan; just count on it."

"Y OU'RE LATE, MISS RAFFA," OLIVER SAID, SHOWING Gloria Raffa into the first-floor living room. "The others have been waiting for over ten minutes."

"I've got a business to run," Gloria said. "I had to give instructions to my staff. And pick out six more outfits; you wouldn't want me to look like Sondra, would you?"

"Try smiling, Gloria," Sondra said. "Just once. I want to see your face crack off."

"This is highly educational," Oliver said smoothly, "and I would love to learn all about your individual faults, but you are taking valuable time away from the others. The contest has already started, officially, and I must explain the house rules."

"You the warden?" Kruger asked.

"I am the butler, sir; you may call me Oliver. And now, if you will follow me . . . ?" He led the way from the living room back to the vestibule door. "Directly adjacent to the front entrance of the first floor is this elevator. Please use it only for going up; the staff will need to make many trips and if they are fatigued, they will be unable to perform perfectly what I require of them. Going down, please use the stairs." He led them up the two steps to the landing of the broad wrought-iron and marble staircase leading to the second floor. "Miss van Broek, of course, may use the elevator on the way down, as well."

"There's nothing wrong with my legs, Mr. Oliver," Victoria said. "It's just my fingers. I'm still pretty spry. I'll walk down like the rest."

"It's just Oliver, Miss van Broek. The staff appreciates your good will, but if you wish . . ."

"This is a beautiful old stair," Richard said. "The white-marble treads and the broad mahogany handrail look very elegant against the gold metalwork."

"You should have seen the main stair in *my* house," Victoria said dreamily. "Daddy's house. It wasn't just a straight run against the wall, like this. It was a *real* staircase, a hollow square in the center of the house, with the steps on three sides and all the upper rooms off passages around the stairwell. When I was a girl, we, all the children, used to lean over the railing and drop tennis balls down the shaft when we saw a servant coming. Right in front of their noses; they used to jump a mile. We also loved to slide down the banister when Daddy was at work. And the first floor . . . It was like a king's castle, with the stair widening out and curving into the ballroom. At my debut, I was dressed all in white, like a real princess . . ." Victoria closed her eyes, entranced by the magic of that beautiful young girl of fifty years ago.

"Yes, Miss Victoria," Oliver said, "it is a most impressive sight. Those of you who wish to see it, as well as the rest of the van Broek mansion, can visit the Cruciverbal Club next week. It has been maintained, for the most part, in its original condition. But in a brownstone such as this one, even though we're wider than most, there is room for only a simple straight run of stairs such as these."

"It looks pretty steep to me," Kruger remarked.

"It is a bit steeper than modern stairs," Oliver said, "because of the limited space available, but it's quite easy to get used to. Just walk on the central carpet runner and slide your hand along the top of the rail for balance."

"There's nothing to hold on to," Victoria said. "The banister is too broad."

"That is only on the first floor, Miss van Broek, for decorative purposes. On the upper floors, there is a full partition along the length of the staircase, so no one can fall over the rail. There is a smaller polished mahogany handrail along the entire stair fixed to that partition. Quite easy to use, I assure you."

"What's downstairs?" Eileen asked. "On the ground floor?"

"That is the service area, Miss Ashe. Actually, it's two steps below sidewalk level. And I regret to say that you are not allowed to enter there. In fact, you are required to confine yourselves to this floor and to the third and fourth floors, your bedroom floors. The fifth floor is the servants' quarters and the second floor is Mr. Sullivan's private area: study, bedroom, and personal guest room. Now, if you will follow me up the stairs..."

"You said we could use the elevator up," Kruger said. "These are high floors and"—he patted his big belly—"I don't like to do any more climbing than I have to. And this banister is too wide for a firm grip. When my bursitis acts up..."

"We can't all fit into the elevator, Mr. Kruger," Oliver said, "but if you have a physical problem, you may ride up with Miss van Broek."

"I'll manage now," Kruger said, "I'm not that bad today. But it's going to get worse; I can tell." They started up the stairs.

"We can't avoid the second floor," Sondra said, "if we have to walk down. We have to go down the main passage along the stair to get to the next set of stairs down. What are we supposed to do, fly?"

"Not at all, Miss Stempel. When you reach the second floor going down, just turn left and walk quietly toward the rear of the house and go down the next flight to the first floor. Follow the path we are now taking, but in reverse. We realize that you must traverse the second floor; the only requirement is that you respect Mr. Sullivan's privacy."

"Can we go anywhere we want to on the first floor?" Victoria asked.

"I'm sorry, Miss van Broek, but the kitchen is also off limits. You realize, of course, that we have eight guests plus Mr. Sullivan which, with our augmented staff, makes seventeen people. It would be too confusing to have any of you in a service area."

"Eight?" Victoria asked. "There are six of us plus Miss Macintosh. That's seven."

"Mrs. Lila Quinn will be staying with us, too, Miss van Broek. Didn't Mr. Sullivan mention her?"

"Sure," Gloria said. "She's the one who'll be running the contest, the crossword maven. But Mr. Sullivan didn't say she'd be staying here. He told us there were three bedrooms on each floor. Where will she be? Will one of us have to double up with her?"

"There is a guest bedroom on the second floor, right at the head of the stairs, Miss Raffa, which is usually available to personal friends of Mr. Sullivan, because the third and fourth floors are kept shut off. Mrs. Quinn will be in that room. You will each have a room to yourselves."

"So Quinn and Macintosh will have to double up?" Sondra said.

"So it appears," Oliver said discreetly.

"I do hope my room won't be musty," Victoria said. "Or dusty. I can't breathe if it is; I can't stand mildew."

"Please be at ease, Miss van Broek. The rooms were thoroughly cleaned twice, professionally, and well aired out. The linens are freshly ironed and the rooms are filled with growing plants."

"What kind?" Victoria asked. "I love cacti, big ones. Several, if there is room."

"The rooms are quite large, Miss Victoria. By this evening, you shall have your wish."

"Can I have cyclamens?" Gloria asked. "In flower, if possible? Especially red. Columbines, too?"

"I'd like a rubber tree or two," Kruger said. "My mother used to have one when I was a boy."

"Please make notes of your personal requirements," Oliver said, "and give them to your floor maid. I will do my best to satisfy your needs. Plants, books, VCR cassettes, beverages, snacks—whatever you desire. A maid is assigned to each floor; she will take care of your needs, anything you ask for. We will all do our best to make your stay most pleasant. Now let us walk up to the third floor."

"It's dark up there," Eileen said.

"Not quite, Miss Ashe; there is always the small light on over the stairs. Since these floors are not normally in use, the main-stair lights are controlled by switches at the head and foot of each stair. As you enter the stair landing the switch is directly on your left. At the head of the stair, the switch is directly to your right, as you go down."

"The corridors are dark," Richard said. "Do the stair switches control the corridor lights, too?"

"The main-stair light spills some light into the corridor; for going up and down, that is sufficient. If you're going to your room, there is a switch at the head of the stair and another next to the elevator, which controls the corridor lights. It shuts itself off after a minute, as do the main-stair lights. And here we are, Miss van Broek. You are at the front of the house on the third floor; less walking that way."

"I think I would prefer the back of the house, Oliver," Victoria said. "I like quiet. I would also prefer to be higher up, too, where it's brighter, and sunny."

"The rear of the house has a southern exposure, Miss van Broek. Sunlight most of the day." Oliver turned to Albert Kruger. "Would you have any objection, sir, to changing with Miss van Broek?"

"Makes no difference to me," Kruger said. "One less flight to walk down."

Oliver turned back to Victoria van Broek. "I will have it taken care of shortly. Now at the rear of this floor I have placed Mr. Deddich near the head of the stair and Miss Ashe in the far rear corner."

"Does that mean that Gloria and Sondra will be on the fourth floor with me?" Victoria asked.

Oliver looked at Gloria Raffa and Sondra Stempel. Gloria shrugged. Sondra made a face, but nodded. "I hope you don't mind being on the fourth floor?" Oliver asked. They both agreed. "Very well, Miss van Broek, I will have your things repacked and moved at once."

"Repacked?" Gloria asked. "The maid went through my things? I have some very expensive jewelry in my bags."

Oliver looked at her coldly. "You are a guest in Mr. Sullivan's home, Miss Raffa. The staff are well aware of their responsibilities." Gloria Raffa stared back at Oliver, unmoved.

Oliver led them toward the front of the house, to the landing of the stair going up. "Let us go up to the fourth floor."

"Is the fourth floor the same as the third?"

"Exactly, madam. Two bedrooms at the rear, one at the front."

"Then you don't have to show us upstairs," Victoria said. "I would appreciate your making up my new room as soon as possible. I'd like to freshen up a bit and take a short rest."

"Very well, madam. I'll go to the floor maids and give them instructions about the new arrangements."

"Is there a phone in my room, Oliver?" Kruger asked. "I have to call my wife."

"There is a phone, sir, but it is only for interior calls. Mr. Sullivan instructed that there was to be no communication with the outside. In case of an emergency, or an unusual requirement, you can reach me at any time, day or night. But even with the extra help, we are not adequately set up as a hotel. I would therefore request that you confine your calls for personal services to the hours between seven A.M. and ten P.M. Breakfast at eight-thirty, lunch at one and dinner at eight. There will be a night man on duty between ten P.M. and seven A.M., but since he is the only one available during those hours, try to keep your calls to him at a minimum. Cleaning and straightening, laundry, ironing, shoe polishing, similar functions, will be done during mealtimes. Are there any questions?"

"Sounds good to me," Kruger said. "Will you have a bottle of single-malt Scotch sent to my room now? No ice."

"I'm sorry, sir. You may have alcoholic beverages one drink at a time, but no bottles. I will have a double Glenfiddich sent to your room shortly. And there is no smoking permitted."

"I'll open the window and blow it outside."

"I'm sorry, sir, but Mr. Sullivan expressly forbids smoking in his house. Your cigars will be returned when you leave." Oliver looked at his watch. "I suggest you all get settled now. We will meet in an hour in Mr. Sullivan's study."

"On the second floor?" Richard asked. "But you said . . ."

"For contest purposes only," Oliver said. "Mrs. Quinn will explain the routine and distribute the first set of puzzles. The study is the room at the rear of the house, away from the stair. Lunch will be served immediately afterward. It will be a buffet today, since we are running somewhat late. And may I wish you all good luck."

8

"**O**KAY," ISABEL SAID, THROWING HER SUITCASE ON THE bed. "Talk. And it better be good."

"Can't we wait until Oliver gets back with the chocolate?" Giles asked. "And what are you doing with that suitcase? Everything's been hung up, you know. As usual," he added hopefully.

"I'm getting ready to pack, Sullivan, in case your explanation is too flimsy for even my trusting nature. I don't want to wait for the chocolate, or anything else, for that matter. In fact, I wouldn't touch a bit of chocolate now even if you put it right in my hand; it might take the edge off—off whatever I decide to do. What I want, Sullivan, is your story. Now. Start lying, Sullivan; I'm waiting."

Giles stood up, straight and tall. "What you're going to get, Macintosh," he said steadily, "is the truth. I've tried to be a gentleman, to avoid embarrassing a lady, but—"

"Are you patronizing me, you—you *Victorian*? I don't need a *protector*; I'm a big girl, and I can take care of myself."

"Protector? Hah! You've been treating me like a—a lackey. Worse. A *cicisbeo*."

"I'm not married, Sullivan, thank God, and if you had had a proper education, you wouldn't have made that mistake. The word you're looking for, given your archaic attitudes is 'leman.'"

"The point is, Macintosh, you were supposed to come *next* Wednesday. Then you call this morning, from the airport, you have to board in thirty seconds, I must pick you up at La Guardia, good-by."

"I cancelled everything, Sullivan, *everything*, because I was dying to see you. A week earlier, yes; I couldn't wait, fool that I was. I thought you'd be overjoyed. Instead I got pained looks, lies about a *little* bit of business, and one lousy chocolate apple. *One*."

"You have some control over your business, Macintosh; I don't. You can assign your duties to subordinates; I can't. There are six heirs, potential heirs, with eighteen million dollars at stake. If I make one tiny mistake . . . You know how many lawyers can be retained to sue for eighteen million dollars? Not just Winston and Harrigan, but me, personally?"

"So it's money now, Sullivan? You don't value me above rubies?"

"I value you above . . . It's not a matter of value, Isabel; I have to make sure *justice* is done. I have to be sure that Cornelius van Broek's brief is carried out faithfully; that the one direct descendant who best exhibits the van Broek characteristics inherits the money."

"That disgusting crew? I'd just as soon give the money to Jack the Ripper."

"He isn't a direct descendant; I have to choose one of those six."

"But only if one of them finds the hidden message. What makes you think that one of them will do it?"

"I hope one will, but I have to prepare for the worst. And I need your help, Isabel."

"To sharpen pencils? To collect papers? I outgrew that level of pedagogy twenty years ago."

"No, Isabel. It will look like that's what you're doing, but you'll actually be watching them; weighing and judging. I can't do it; they'll be on their best behavior when I'm around."

"You'd trust *my* judgment on this, Sullivan? Really? Risk your reputation, your money, Winston and Harrigan, on my opinion?"

"I'm willing to put my life in your hands, Isabel; why not this?"

"Keep talking, Giles; you're beginning to sound like Cary Grant. A little."

"I *am* overjoyed that you're here, Isabel; the time we spend apart is worse for me than it is for you. My life is completely empty, meaningless, when you're not at my side. That's why I was so pleased I could fit you into these arrangements, arrangements I could not change. I am happiest when we work together, when we're in harness together. Please forgive the situation—it was truly unavoidable—and let's make the best of it. Together."

"Oh, Giles, when you talk like that, I could—take the entire blame for your stupidities on myself. Lock the door and kiss me."

"I'm sorry, darling, but we have to meet Lila Quinn and the six heirs in the study right now, to give out the first puzzles, and we're already late. But we can skip lunch..."

"Okay, I'll bend with the wind. Just let me put my suitcase into the closet and— Where's the rest of my clothes? There are only a few things here."

"Oh," Giles said lightly, moving to the door, "I forgot to tell you. I don't want the heirs to get the idea that you and I are particularly close. It would be much better if they saw us as—as arms-length colleagues. That way, the losers can't claim collusion on our part. You'll be sleeping with Lila Quinn, in the back bedroom."

9

"**I** WOULD LIKE EACH OF YOU"—LILA QUINN PLACED THE big manila envelope on the desk before her—"to examine this carefully before I open it. Please pay particular attention to the seals and the signatures across the flap."

"Why all the formality?" Kruger asked. "Just open it and pass out the puzzles."

"Don't be in such a hurry, sonny," Lila said calmly. "You don't like the way I do things, go home. There's going to be one winner and five losers, and I don't want any of you to sue me when you lose. Neither does Mr. Sullivan. There's a magnifying glass for whoever wants to use it."

Victoria van Broek put on her reading glasses and leaned over the envelope. "That's Daddy's seal, all right, and his signature across the flap. I know."

"I had three handwriting experts," Giles said, "verify the signatures on all three envelopes, and two laboratories agreed that the envelopes had never been opened."

"I'll accept that they're genuine," Richard said, "subject to seeing the reports."

"We'll meet here," Lila said, "every day at noon. I'll collect your previous day's test and pass out the next one." She put another paper on the table. "All of you sign this agreement that you accept the rules and decisions of the judge. That's me. I'm completely disinterested; I don't give a damn who wins."

"I always have my lawyer check anything I sign," Gloria said.

"Good. I'll make a copy for you on the machine. Take it to your lawyer and, when he's made his changes, have him call Mr. Winston, who will make his own changes to the changes. A year from now, he may approve your signing on the dotted line. Only trouble is, this contest is over in one week, maximum." Lila smiled at Gloria. "So? Decide, Raffa.

Sign or get out. Don't forget, when you sue, you'll be suing the winner to take away his eighteen million, which he can use to fight you. For that much dough, you can hire an awful lot of lawyers. Then you've got to fight me, Giles Sullivan, and Winston and Harrigan. I'll give you a tip, lady; that way you've got one chance in a million. If you take the test, you've got one chance in six. So?"

"Better than one in six, Quinn," Gloria said. "When it comes to words, I'm one of the best in New York. Hollywood, too. I'll sign. But you watch how you talk to me, Quinn. After the contest is over, win or lose, I still have plenty of clout in this town."

"I'm scared to death, Raffa. At my age, what can you do to me that hasn't already been done? And will you note the attitude of contestant Gloria Raffa, Miss Macintosh? I mean, just in case nobody solves the problem and we have to decide who has Cornelius van Broek's style. Would he have threatened somebody who holds his fate in her hands?"

"He was too smart for that, Mrs. Quinn," Giles said solemnly. Lila patted her dyed-blond bouffant exaggeratedly. "Anyone else want to give me any lip?" She looked around the room. "No? Okay. The next step is, you all sign this envelope."

"Before it's opened?" Eileen asked.

"That's right, Eileen. Not near the end, please. This envelope, with your signatures on it, goes into the vault." They all lined up and signed.

Lila carefully scissored the end of the envelope off and took out the pack of papers, face down. "Okay, kids, each of you sign the back of this sheet."

"My God," Kruger said, "do we have to go through this every time?"

"You got anything better to do, sonny? If you have, name it; maybe I'll join you. Of course, if you all just shut up and do what you have to do, we can go through the procedure in one minute." Under the lash of Lila's sharp tongue, they signed the back of the sheet.

"Miss Macintosh, take this sheet, two fingers, keep it in full sight all the time, and make fifteen copies of it on the copier."

"Fifteen copies?" Victoria asked. "There are only six of us."

"You each get one extra to make mistakes on. The other three are for me, Sullivan, and Macintosh to play with. Now I'm going to turn over the puzzle you signed on the back and spread out the batch of copies. See that they're the same."

"They're all the same," Eileen said.

"Take two copies each, go back to your rooms, and solve the puzzle." Lila looked at her puzzle for a moment. "Which should take a few minutes although, since these were made in 1935, you younger ones are at a disadvantage. But you have plenty of time, so check your references to make sure."

"What references?" Eileen asked.

Lila waved at the floor-to-ceiling shelves of books lining the study. "These references."

"Oliver said we couldn't go to any room on this floor," Richard said. "How do we get the references?"

"You'll find most of what you need on your desks. A good lamp, fine-line pens—yes, I know, thick-bodied pens for you, Miss van Broek—pencils, an electric sharpener, and some basic references that should take care of almost all your needs."

"What if we need more?"

"Just phone me or Miss Macintosh; whatever you need will be sent to your room from here. In fact, knowing that the puzzles were made in the thirties, we ordered some dictionaries and other references from that period. Nothing is too good for our contestants."

"But we don't know what books you have here," Eileen said.

"Just tell me the kind of book you want; I'll get you the right one. And just in case anyone tries to be a wise guy and hog all the books on a certain subject, a limit of five books out at a time. But believe me, this puzzle looks like a snap. The hard part has got to be the hidden message. Any questions?"

"What do we do after we've solved the puzzle?" Sondra asked.

"Make a neat, clear copy, in ink, sign it, and give it to me when you pick up the next puzzle. Isabel Macintosh will make a copy of your puzzle on the machine, and she and I will sign it for your records. Your original submission goes into an envelope, sealed, and the three of us sign across the flap. Then we put it in the safe."

"What do I do when I find the hidden message?" Victoria asked.

"I don't know," Lila admitted. "I figure the message has to tell you that. One more thing. In case any of you are rusty, or want a refresher, right after lunch Miss Macintosh and I will give a short lesson in speed-solving techniques. In the living room. All welcome."

"I don't think I need any help," Victoria said. "Thank you."

"I'll stand pat, too," Kruger said.

"Nobody?" Lila asked, looking around. "Okay, then. Go down to the dining room; there'll be a buffet lunch. Late, but good. After lunch, go to your rooms, solve the puzzle, find the message, and get rich. And good luck." She didn't sound a bit sincere.

10

"WHEN DID YOU TURN INTO ATTILA THE HUN?" ISABEL asked, spreading the tablecloth over the cleared desk and distributing the sandwiches Oliver had brought up to the study. "The last time I saw you, you were a nice Jewish grandmother from Brooklyn. And why didn't we eat with the six heirs? I wanted to observe them in a relaxed atmosphere."

"By my grandchildren," Lila said, "I'm still nice. But with this bunch of *momzers* ... I figured, if I cracked the whip early, they'd know not to start anything. Let Oliver observe them now; you can observe them at supper. We have things to talk about."

"What could they start, Lila?" Giles asked. "I've got everything so organized that there is no way for anyone to cheat."

"The New York City government is also organized, Giles; that's why it's so easy to cheat them. When you were a criminal lawyer, you didn't learn this?"

"I've got them all under one roof, Lila, in separate rooms, with no way to communicate with the outside. The lowest bedroom is three stories above street level. They didn't even know they were going to be here until the last moment, and they were fully supervised after that."

Lila looked at Isabel in disbelief. "He really believes that?" Isabel nodded. Lila shook her head. "You tell him, Isabel; I don't have the heart."

"If I wanted to sneak out at midnight for a date with Cary Grant," Isabel said, "I wouldn't risk getting a run in my stockings by jumping from a third-floor window. I'd just walk down to the first floor like a lady and out the front door."

"I have a night man on duty," Giles said. "I'll instruct him to stay near the family entrance. That way he can watch the elevator and the first-floor stair landing as well."

"That makes things really difficult for me, Sullivan. Now I have to take the elevator all the way down to the ground floor and use the service entrance to get out."

"The elevator sometimes makes noise. If the night man hears it..."

"*If*. But let's say I don't even want to risk that. I'll just have my confederate on the fourth floor, the one I'm going to split my winnings with, order some barley water and a hot-water bottle. While the night man is fumbling around in the ground-floor service area, I glide down the marble staircase like a princess."

"I'm not worried," Lila said, "that one of our internees will sneak out and put an ad for a cryptanalyst in the *Daily News*. Our problem isn't even collusion—"

"Not *even* collusion?" Giles exploded. "I've made sure there's no way anyone can get a penny by cheating."

"If I were an heir," Lila said, "the first thing I'd do is make a deal with Victoria. Cornelius was a businessman, born in Holland. No matter how good his English was, he had to have used a very simple method to hide his message. Who better than Victoria to read his mind of fifty years ago?"

"She must know that, so what does she gain by making a deal?"

"Aside from doubling her chances, I'd tell her that I had found the message but didn't understand what it meant. And I wanted something in writing to guarantee I got my share."

"Exactly, Lila. If you tried to use that contract, you'd both lose the money."

"Not a contract; a will. Leaving all the money to her collaborator. After all, how much longer could she live?"

"She can change her will," Giles said, "the day after she gets the money. The collaborator is completely unprotected."

"He knows that. So right after Victoria turns in the winning answer..."

"In *my* house? He'd *kill* her?"

"It's happened before, Giles. Harvey Brundage, remember?"

Giles thought for a moment. "If we have to consider that, what's to stop...? The will provides that the direct descendant who most *closely* matches the van Broek characteristics inherits everything. If there were only one heir left . . ." Giles picked up the phone.

Isabel put her hand on the bar. "What are you doing?"

"Calling Oliver. It's a buffet lunch. Anyone could put anything into a platter. I could have five dead people on my head. More. The servants eat the same food."

"It won't happen today, Giles," Isabel said. "First, he or she—don't forget that poison is a woman's weapon—will want to study one crossword, at least. Second, she's not going to kill five at once and leave only herself alive; you might decide she lacks character and doesn't deserve to inherit. One at a time is more like it. No, mass murder is not the problem; at least not today."

"I can't change the arrangements now, Isabel. If I did, I could be sued, and rightly, to void the results. There could be claims that the change, any change, was favoritism, or that it upset this or that contestant so that he could not function properly. But I can't let him commit murder either. What am I to do?"

"First," Lila said, "we finish eating. Then let's do the first crossword and find the message."

"What for?" Giles asked. "We can't win."

"The message might be a clue, might tell us who to watch carefully; who knows? What could it hurt? It won't take long and it could be fun. Better than talking to those creeps."

"You haven't made any concrete suggestions, Lila, as to how to handle this problem."

"Oh, that's easy, Giles." She showed her teeth in her blitz-Scrabble hustler's smile. "Take out more insurance, Giles, lots of it. Fast."

ACROSS

1 Obstruct
4 Rough, as an uncut
   diamond
8 Swiss mountain
11 Expression of pity
13 Loud
14 Food in general
16 Am. painter, Rockwell ___
17 Toward the center
18 Poison
19 Wrested by violence
21 Citrus fruit
23 Tall marsh stalk
24 Record of a ship's voyage
25 St. Francis ___
28 Traveler's guidebook
33 Biblical name
34 Batsman's side (Cricket)
35 Bird related to the ostrich
36 Horses (Colloq.)
37 Selected

39 Bad; harmful
40 Shoulder (Pref.)
41 Cereal grass
42 Spigot
43 Region of N.W. France
46 Polished
47 Sprite
48 Outer garment
49 Hard, glossy, dental layer
52 Language of Syria and
   Mesopotamia
56 Beast's leg (Her.)
57 Bring upon one's self
59 Ship's mast
60 Banter; deride
61 Small ropes
62 Detest
63 In place of
64 Woody plant
65 Incline the head

DOWN

1 Cook in an oven
2 Man's nickname
3 Declaim violently
4 Having a skeleton
5 Thick skin
6 Employ
7 Of an Alpine province, W.
   Austria
8 Circumlocution
9 Incline
10 Twinge of pain
12 Tales
13 Saltpeter
15 Starting place (Golf)
20 Spool
22 16½ feet
25 Gaseous element
26 Building in San Antonio,
   Texas
27 Active strength
28 Spoils taken, as in war

29 Reply (Abbr.)
30 Irish man's name
31 ___ Zola
32 Governed
37 Prolonged struggle
38 Owned
39 Tombstone inscription
42 Trick; hoax
44 Constituent part
45 Light-colored beer
46 Flies upward
48 Raw; unprepared
49 Ovum
50 Artless
51 Raised pulpit
52 160 square rods
53 Of the dawn
54 Countertenor
55 Necessity
58 Correlative of "neither"

Puzzle No. 1

"THIS ONE WAS A SNAP," LILA SAID. "WHAT KEPT YOU?"

"I wasn't trying for speed," Giles alibied, putting down his pen. "I was looking for a pattern."

"Shut up," Isabel said. "I'm not used to old-fashioned puzzles like this, and I wasn't even able to read when this puzzle was made."

"I wish I could say that," Lila said enviously. "I'd trade half my vocabulary to be fifty-five again. If I could look like you, Isabel."

"Leaving you with a lousy hundred thousand words? You'd be practically speechless, Lila."

"If I looked like you, Izzy, I could get along very pleasurably with three words, a grunt, and a couple of moans. Knowing a twelve-letter word for 'perhaps' doesn't provide a hell of a lot of warmth on a cold winter's night."

"Don't say that, Lila. In the long run, it's character that counts."

"It's the flower that attracts the bee, honey; until that happens, he doesn't know from character. What do you say, Giles? Find anything in this tedious, tiresome, boring, uninteresting, bland, insipid, jejune—how's that for vocabulary, Isabel; want to trade your looks for my brains—dull puzzle?"

"Well, you must understand, Lila, that Cornelius van Broek was not a professional constructor. I think we can excuse a certain lack of wit and humor."

"Sure, Giles, a *certain* lack. But *so much* lack? I don't care what others say about unfair; I'd love a puzzle by Hannibal right now, just to get my glands working again." She looked straight into Giles's eyes. "You wouldn't happen to have one lying around, would you?"

"Nothing, Lila. Not one. Let's get back to this puzzle.

See any pattern? Consistencies? Regularities?"

"Well, I did see something at four Across. 'BRUT,' today, refers to champagne; means very dry. I never heard of his clue."

"Maybe he means '*bort*,'" Isabel said. "Industrial diamonds."

"I don't think so," Giles said. "Cornelius was a very unimaginative type, a conformist. I'm sure if we looked it up in a dictionary of that time, his definition would hold."

"So look it up, Giles; I'm always trying to increase my vocabulary. Just in case the devil makes me an offer, you understand: fifty thousand words for fifty years. Of age, I mean. Or even five years. Anybody listening? I'm serious."

"It's not worth the effort of looking it up, Lila; the accuracy of the puzzle is not what counts, it's the message."

"I did notice," Isabel said, "there was a large number of geographical references: 'ALP,' 'BAEDEKER,' 'NORMANDY,' 'TYROLESE,' 'ALAMO.' And if you stretch things a bit, you could add: 'BAR,' 'KENT,' 'EMU,' 'ARAMAEAN,' 'POLE,' 'ROD,' and 'ACRE.' Then there's 'XAVIER,' 'ELIEL,' 'KEVIN,' and 'EMILE.'"

"I saw that, too," Lila said. "But try putting them together in a message."

"Just thought I'd mention it. What about standard patterns, Giles? A Stepquote type, maybe?"

"Going from one to two and down in steps, we get 'BALANTOREER-OOS-SHATAEOLTED.' I don't see any message there."

"How about starting one to eleven and then across," Isabel said. "'BALENTOREER-HAT-SOAMAPOATOD.' That's very unusual, the first group of letters is almost exactly the same as in the set you picked."

"It is unusual, Isabel, but there is some justification for it. In a Stepquote from upper left to lower right, it doesn't matter if you go across or down from box one, you still hit all the diagonal letters, 'B-L-N-O-E-R' and so forth. But this puzzle is unusual in that four of the five sets of letters adjacent to the diagonal are the same: A-A, T-T, R-R, and E-E. Let's look at those two groups, 'BALANTOREER' and 'BALENTOREER' and see if there is a message there." He studied the letters carefully for several minutes. "Nope, I see nothing. You, Lila?"

"Not a thing. I've also checked lower left to upper right. Dead."

"How about the diagonals?" Isabel asked. "You see anything, Giles?"

"'BLNOER-O-SAAOTD'? Even the other way, 'AAA-OENOANLMMI.' Nothing."

"Wait," Isabel said. "The interior diagonal square. Like the one in Washington? Look, it's clear all the way around."

"You had a will in Washington, too?" Lila asked.

"Oh, no," Giles said quickly. "We were on vacation"—Isabel choked down a bitter laugh—"and we saw some Washington puzzles. You start at the middle of the top line Across and follow a diagonal around counter-clockwise to form a square tilted at forty-five degrees to the main square of the puzzle. Starting at box five, it reads: 'ROIRRVLN-MREEIOE-DRMTNLL-MKGRRS.' Doesn't look like a message to me. What do you think, Lila?"

"I don't see anything, but then, I'm a crossword solver, not a code breaker."

"Let's try working right to left on each side of the tilted square," Isabel said, "the way we did in Washington. We get: 'ROIRRVLN-EOIEERM-LLNTMRO-MKGRRS.' You see anything, Giles?"

He shook his head resignedly. "I don't think so. But more important, I think we're getting too complex. Cornelius van Broek was a simple man, a one-plus-one-equals-two type. The message has to be simple, and it has to be concealed simply. Let's try word combinations. Or are there any other patterns you see, Lila?"

"Well, there's a high concentration of food words, especially if you count animals, too: 'MEAT,' 'ORANGE,' 'EMU,' 'NAGS,' 'OAT,' 'GAMB,' 'BAKE,' 'BONED,' 'RIND,' 'ALE,' and 'EGG.' If you want to stretch things a bit, 'BAR' is the way some people pronounce 'BEAR', 'BRUT' as in champagne, 'OMO' for shoulder, 'SPILE' for spigot, 'ENAMEL' for teeth to eat with, 'LEAN' for lean meat, 'PANG' for hunger pangs, 'NITER' for curing meat, and 'REEL' and 'ROD' for catching fish."

"That's a very large number, Lila, but I don't see any pattern."

"Maybe there isn't a pattern, Giles."

"There must be. Cornelius wouldn't play tricks."

"Suppose," Isabel said thoughtfully, "we had to have the whole set of puzzles to put together before the message became clear. Isn't that what the will says?"

"I've memorized the key instructions," Giles said. "'. . . a series of crossword puzzles which, when solved, will provide the message which leads to the inheritance. When you have all the words written down, the key will appear.'"

"There, Giles, a *series* of crosswords. 'When you have *all* the words written down . . .' We haven't done all the crosswords yet, the whole series."

"I don't think you're right, Isabel. In solving a puzzle, unless you do it in your head, you automatically write down *all* the words. There may be three separate parts to the message, three messages, but each part should yield *something*."

"Maybe we're overlooking something, Giles," Lila said. "The instruction said; '. . . will provide the message which *leads* to the inheritance.' Maybe the message isn't in words, but describes a path. What would happen if—remember the geographical names?—if we plotted those locations on a map, a Mercator projection? Or a globe?"

"Well, we can try it," Giles said, taking a large atlas down from a high shelf. "The Tyrolean Alps, Normandy, the Alamo, Kent, Syria. Nope, nothing there. Too few points. Isolated points. I don't see any pattern, do you? Even if we treat 'POLE' as Poland?"

"We need a lot more points on the map," Lila said, "if it's to make a recognizable pattern. Let's see what the next puzzle shows."

Isabel stood up. "Enough of this. I've been going from early this morning. I need a shower and a nap."

"Okay, Isabel," Lila said. "I'll stay here on duty and ring you if I need any help."

"Ring me in our room."

"Sure, I know."

"I mean yours and mine, Lila."

"But I thought . . ."

"You thought wrong, Lila. Giles needs his privacy for administrating and for maturing his felonious little plans. See you at supper, Giles. Call me if you find the hidden message, and for anything really important. Like murder. *Nothing* else."

"ANYTHING OF INTEREST TO REPORT, OLIVER?" GILES asked. Oliver was watching the new scullery maid/waitress, a plump gray-haired woman, clearing the table.

"Only idiosyncratic evidence, sir. Mr. Kruger ate some of everything, even though he seemed completely stuffed near the end of the meal. Miss van Broek ate heartily, but only of the most costly dishes. Miss Raffa ate very sparingly, with an eye on the lowest caloric values, though she did take a taste of every dessert, and a second taste of Ping's chocolate ice cream."

"Is there any left, Oliver? You didn't send any up to us in the study."

"Ping's special ice cream does not travel well, sir. I put out a measured amount for our guests and left one container for the servants and another container in the freezer for your personal use, sir. It is on its way to your room right now, sir. If you hurry, Miss Isabel may not have finished it all by the time you get there."

"But she's not—."

"Gina was instructed to deliver it to Miss Isabel directly. One container, two spoons. So that you may eat very slowly, a visible act of contrition that is sure to be appreciated, and thus achieve absolution."

"Thank you, Oliver, but I must first know about the others."

"Miss Ashe ate a great deal of the salads, most surprising for such a slim young woman. Mr. Deddich decided which food he preferred, usually the blandest dish which most closely resembled the conventional, and ate that one item in each course. Miss Stempel selected the spiciest dishes and overcrowded her plate. Leaving half the food on her plate, she went back and filled a new plate. A disturbing exhibition, if I may say so, sir."

"Yes, of course, Oliver, but what I'm really interested in is—were there any signs of...? Mrs. Quinn thinks, feels, that one of them may decide to..."

"I did think of that, sir, although it would be most unlikely at the lunch buffet. I took no part in the serving, but stationed myself at the end of the buffet and watched the hands. I saw nothing even slightly suspicious. If there is to be an attempt at foul play, sir, I do not think it will be in the dining room. With all their faults, our guests are quite intelligent."

"Where would it be, Oliver?"

"In the privacy of the victim's room, sir. That way, no one other than the murderer could observe anything, and the body would not be discovered until the next day, which would increase the probability of blurring the exact time of death."

"You mean at night, Oliver?"

"Less chance of being observed accidentally, sir. The night-duty man will be stationed near the front door, two or three floors down."

"But at night, Oliver? The heirs will all be behind their locked doors, busy working, trying to solve the problem, to find the hidden message. None of them would let anyone into his room after ten. Or even before. I mean, if he has his papers spread out on his desk and one of his relations, competitors actually, knocks on the door, the proper answer would be, 'Go away.'"

"Miss Ashe is a very attractive young lady, sir; it would be difficult for any man to send her away. Mr. Deddich has the air of a young man who has not socialized with women very much. I would judge him to be quite vulnerable. Mr. Kruger, too, I feel, would not be averse to a bit of dalliance in a situation where his wife could not possibly surprise him."

"I take your point, Oliver. Very well, then, station Agnes and Carmen with orders not to permit—"

"I'm sorry, sir, but the maids will be on duty from seven in the morning until ten at night. Even if they were willing, it is improbable that they would be maximally alert at three A.M."

"Then hire two more—"

"We cannot deviate from the original arrangements, sir, as you so strongly impressed on me when I raised certain cavils before."

"Then Eileen may be in a position to . . . But she's so young, Oliver."

"My collection of whodunits is replete with instances of beautiful young ladies who killed aged relatives in order to inherit much smaller fortunes. But you should not think only of Miss Ashe, sir. Miss Stempel is only slightly older than Mr. Deddich."

"But she's decidedly unattractive, Oliver."

"There is no accounting for taste, sir. To a person as inexperienced as Mr. Deddich appears to be, a young woman of Miss Stempel's high spirits might promise untold delights. But we should not limit ourselves to Mr. Deddich alone. You may remember I told you Mr. Kruger sampled some of each dish? Miss Stempel might very well represent a new experience for him."

"My God, Oliver, do you realize what you're saying? We could have them dashing through the corridors like a Feydeau farce."

"Miss Raffa is quite attractive in a mature way. Mr. Kruger went out of his way to converse with her during lunch. She could easily turn the head of an introverted young man, too."

"But they're all related to each other. It would be . . ."

"Incest, sir? Yes, sir, although some of the relationships are quite distant. But if one intends to commit murder, sir, would a bit of incest stand in the way?"

Giles shook his head wearily. "I see now that I should have given it over completely to an outside agency. But it seemed such an ideal fit." He drew a deep breath. "Well, at least Victoria van Broek won't be involved."

"I am sorry to disillusion you, sir, but Miss van Broek is not immune either."

"Isn't she rather . . . ?"

"Poor people do tend to be unattractive, sir. But I had Carmen get the size of her clothes and I took the liberty of ordering several complete new outfits for her. I am sure she will be pleased and, if she is not the winner, the memory of looking like a queen for a week will warm her declining years. At dinner you may observe the transformation."

"It takes a certain attitude, Oliver, as well as clothes."

"I am aware of that, sir. But in Miss van Broek's youth, particularly after her father's death, she was known in the gossip columns as 'The Madcap Heiress.'"

"I take your point, Oliver. You are telling me that I have to watch all six of them. Worry about the whole bunch. There are, let me see, seven possible combinations to consider. Perhaps we should just concentrate on the two men."

"Not necessarily, sir. These days, there seem to be several more divisions of the human race than there were when I was a boy. If one or more of the ladies are experimentally inclined, and one or more of the men, we expand to a very large number of possible connections. That is, sir, if we consider them only in twos."

"My God, Oliver, who would think that people of that age..."

"Quite, sir. But may I point out that Miss Isabel would rightfully be considered a mature person, as measured by years, and her actions, at times, though highly entertaining, have, in the past, caused you some concern." Oliver glanced at his watch. "I suggest you hurry upstairs, sir, before Ping's special ice cream is completely melted."

13

"**I** KNOCKED ON THE DOOR OF LILA'S ROOM," GILES explained, "and there was no answer, so I came here."

"I'm used to this bed, Sullivan. No sense in tossing and turning, using all the time I allotted for a short nap, in not sleeping."

"You ate all the ice cream, too? Ping's special chocolate? The whole container?"

"Half air, to begin with. And it was melting. While you were wasting time on whatever business you thought was more important than hurrying back here."

"But I had to ... Didn't Oliver get you some other chocolate?"

"One day's supply. That wasn't melting, so I'm saving it for later. Shows self-control. From my New England upbringing."

"Sure, Macintosh, for which you are justly famous. Aren't you going to ask me what I found out?"

"We're living in a den of potential murderers. So what else is new?"

"How did you ... ?"

"Even Agatha Christie knew that if you put six people on a desert island and the survivor gets eighteen million dollars, one of them, if they're normal human beings, is going to try to knock off the other five."

"But at the time, I didn't think—"

"For which *you* are justly famous, Sullivan. You're certain that everyone is as honest and straightforward as you are."

"I had only the best of motives, Macintosh."

"Why don't you consult me, Sullivan, before you take moronic action?"

"It was a perfectly sensible arrangement, Macintosh."

"Sure, and I didn't know the gun was loaded. And you

talk too much, did anyone ever tell you that?"

"But I thought . . ."

"Do you really think I should be deprived of *my* pleasure because of *your* cloddishness? Is that your idea of justice? Make believe you're a gentleman and take your shoes off first. And stop talking. Completely. Unless you can remember what I told you Cary Grant used to say to me at moments like these."

"**H**AVE YOU HURT YOUR FOOT, MR. SULLIVAN?" EILEEN asked. The nine of them, Isabel, Lila, and Giles, and the six contesting heirs, were seated around the extended dining-room table. Oliver had set out the best service, silver, china, and crystal, in the hope that the formal display, and its implicit requirements of gentility, would still the savage beast, awakened by the scent of eighteen million dollars, that stirred, so near the surface, in the breast of each of their guests.

Oliver had instructed Ping to prepare a truly elegant meal, and Ping had complied enthusiastically, reliving his golden days at the Savoy. Oliver himself served the table, assisted by Ping's neatly aproned-and-capped scullery maid.

Giles sat at the head of the table, Isabel at the foot. On his right was Victoria van Broek, looking queenly in her new evening gown, touched by the unaccustomed wines, cheeks glowing in the light of the tall, slim white candles. To her right sat Albert Kruger, belt loosened prophylactically, and on his right was Gloria Raffa, her makeup a bit too hard for the yellow candle glow. On Giles's left was Sondra Stempel, red hair tied back, looking a little less frumpy than before, torn between the need to denounce the luxury and her naked desire to wallow in it. On her left Richard Deddich sat demurely, his eyes fixed on Giles's plate so as to be certain of using the right fork. Next to him Eileen Ashe shone white and gold, looking like a child allowed to sit at the grownups' table for the first time, beautiful in her youth. Between her and Isabel, Lila Quinn sat, openly staring at the six heirs. Oliver served the crudités, the raw, crunchy vegetables, with a cruet of oil and vinegar dressing.

"My foot?" Giles asked. "There's nothing wrong with my foot."

"Oh, but I thought—" Eileen sounded flustered. "In Winston's office you had your cane with you, but when we were in your study today before lunch, you didn't. So I thought you just used it for out-of-doors. But you have it now, so I assumed that you had twisted your ankle or something."

"No, no," Giles covered up. "I always carry it, just in case—I have an old—the war, you know—and sometimes it acts up." He slipped the cane under the table, next to his chair, within easy reach. Isabel gave him a dirty look.

"Daddy always carried a cane when he left the house," Victoria said. "And he always wore a hat outdoors, even in summer. And spats. He was so very elegant in his dress. Even in the house. Never in shirt-sleeves; he had a smoking jacket."

"Yes, well, in those days," Giles added, "it was accepted that gentlemen of a certain age and class dressed a certain way. Tell me, Miss van Broek, what did you think of the first crossword?"

Hazel began removing the plates, and Oliver served artichoke hearts with drawn butter sauce.

"Exactly as I expected, Mr. Sullivan. Not very difficult, and rather dull. No wit, no humor, a rigid pattern. Just like Daddy. He was very serious, you know."

"And the message? The hidden message?"

"Oh, I didn't even think of that," Victoria said lightly. "I was too busy trying on my new clothes. They're perfect, Mr. Sullivan, thank you. You have very good taste."

"Who are you kidding, Aunt Victoria?" Kruger said roughly. "Still trying to fool everybody? You've been working on the message all afternoon, like everybody else, and you think you've found something. You're trying to hide it. Why? You think we'd try to steal it? What makes you so sure you're right?"

"The thought never entered my mind," Victoria said, "because I don't have to think about the message. I know how Daddy thought; that's enough. I'm just going to follow his directions, and the key will appear to me."

"You're telling me," Kruger ground out, "that I don't have to figure anything at all? Just finish the three puzzles and then I'll automatically know the message?"

"*You* won't, Albert, but I will. You wouldn't recognize the message if it was put right in front of your nose, but it will be perfectly clear to me."

"Stop turning blue, Albert," Gloria said, "that's typical Vickie. Can't you see she's doing it just to get your goat? If you want to get a stroke... On second thought, darling, go right ahead and put yourself out of the running; it's okay by me."

Oliver served the billi-bi, hot cream of mussel soup.

"Great-Aunt Victoria is right," Eileen said. "The will clearly said *after* you put *all* the words down. You can't do that until Friday."

"Why do we have to wait till Friday, Mr. Sullivan?" Richard asked. "Nothing in the will— I read my copy this afternoon—says anything about getting the puzzles a day apart."

"It does say that I am to conduct the test in a way that insures that everyone has a fair chance," Giles replied. "This is not supposed to be a speed-solving contest or a thirties trivia contest. Patience was also one of Cornelius van Broek's virtues, and I am, quite frankly, using this time to observe how each of you reacts to the circumstances of these tests."

"That penalizes those of us who work fast," Sondra complained.

"It's the same for everyone," Giles said. "If you solve the puzzles quickly, you have more time to look for the hidden message."

"Did you solve the puzzle, Mr. Sullivan?" Eileen asked.

"Well, yes I did."

"And you left the solved puzzle on the desk? In your study?"

"Well, yes, of course."

"Your study door, is it locked?"

"I'm not accustomed to... In my own home? My own guests? Are you suggesting...? That would be completely useless. The puzzle was not very hard. I'm sure all of you have solved it already." Lila pushed her chair back and quietly walked to the stairs.

Oliver served the sauteed crabmeat and capers, with potato puffs and braised leeks. He filled the wineglasses with a pale Muscadet.

"I'm sure everyone solved the puzzle," Eileen said. "I certainly had no trouble with it. But I wasn't thinking of that, Mr. Sullivan. If every guest in your own home is so trustworthy, why are you taking such extreme precautions? Maybe for eighteen million dollars, normally trustworthy people might lower their standards a little? You also looked for the hidden message, didn't you, Mr. Sullivan?"

"I didn't find it, Miss Ashe, so there's no point in stealing my notes."

"Great-Aunt Victoria isn't the only one here who knew how my great-grandfather thought, is she? You knew him quite well, Mr. Sullivan, didn't you? Possibly your failures, false starts, will show an approach none of us thought of."

Giles flushed. "Mrs. Quinn has just gone upstairs to lock the study door."

"Oh?" Eileen lifted her eyebrows. "Then you were in the study until just before you came down to dinner? You changed your clothes in the study?"

"I—no, not really. I left the study sometime before."

"Then anyone who wanted to could have just walked into the study, Mr. Sullivan, sat at your desk, and studied, or even copied, on your own copier, your notes on the hidden message?" Giles didn't respond. "How long were you out of the study, Mr. Sullivan? What were you doing that was so much more important than making sure no one got an unfair advantage over me?"

Isabel stood up, her face red. "Shut up, Miss Ashe. You, all of you, have no idea how hard it is to set up a test of this kind, even if every contestant is honest. Yes, it is possible that one of you sneaked into the study while Giles was out of it. It never occurred to him that a guest would pull a rotten trick like that. But it wasn't done. No way."

"How do you know?" Richard asked.

Lila came back to the table, visibly upset. Isabel motioned her to sit down and addressed Richard. "There are some things you don't know, Deddich. Lila was in the study all afternoon, prepared to give out reference books. Did you get any calls, Lila?"

"None, the puzzle was pretty easy."

"So you see," Isabel continued, "no one could have sneaked into the study. But from now on, all notes will be kept in the safe, and the study door locked."

"So Mrs. Quinn changed her clothes in the study?" Eileen asked. She turned to Lila. "How long were you out of the study, Mrs. Quinn? How long did it take you to wash, dress, make up? Weren't you out of the study just before dinner? It's just a few steps from the head of the stairs to the study;

I know, because the study is directly under my room. Do you have the combination to the safe, Mrs. Quinn?"

Lila's face remained blank. Oliver served the pear-frangipane tart and poured coffee.

Eileen studied Lila's face, then continued. "I thought not, Mrs. Quinn. You just shoved the papers into the desk drawer, in a room which can be opened with a credit card." She turned to Giles. "Don't rush upstairs to put your notes in the safe; after dinner would be just as good. Provided you get up there before any of my dear relatives do."

"The way you talk about your relatives, Miss Ashe"— Isabel smiled, too sweetly—"also describes you. I don't think any of you fit Cornelius van Broek's requirements. If there is any justice, the Boy Scouts will inherit the money."

Eileen stood up and smiled back at Isabel. "Whoever finds the message wins the money, Miss Macintosh, and there's nothing you can do about it." She started to sit down, then rose again. "To my dear family: Don't try to find *my* notes. I'll be carrying them with me all the time. And anyone who tries to get into my room uninvited will find a letter opener in his guts before he can say: 'Oops, sorry, wrong room.'" She pushed the tart away. "I don't want anything served to me that smells like almonds. And if my coffee starts tasting funny, I'll make sure one of you drinks it first if I have to pour it down your throat." Eileen Ashe no longer looked like a nice little girl.

15

"BUT WHY, LILA," GILES ASKED, "WHY DID YOU TELL Oliver not to wake me?" He and Isabel were sitting in front of the big desk in the study, Lila in the swivel chair behind it like a schoolmistress. "Why did I have to stay in my room all morning? And why can't we eat lunch with the others?"

"First of all, Giles," Lila replied, "I'm running this contest, not you. That's what you promised me when I took the job. You also forgot to mention what a lousy bunch of creeps they were—God, the things I do for money—so I not only have to worry about cheating, I got to watch out for one of them slipping a knife into another one's back. Then, you didn't tell me how much money was involved. *Eighteen million.* Unbelievable. You should have seen them when I gave out Puzzle Number Two; like a pack of starving wolves."

"I didn't know anything about their characters, Lila, when I made the arrangements; all I had were the dossiers. I didn't mention the amount of the inheritance because I didn't think it was important."

"Not important? When I was a girl, Giles, you could get a guy knocked off by a top professional for a lousy grand. Less. For eighteen million you could get twenty *thousand* people killed, wholesale rates. Did old Cornelius have any idea of what this inheritance would do to his direct descendants?"

"I doubt it, Lila. First of all, he really couldn't conceive that it would turn into eighteen million; the effect of the wars—he died in '42, you know—the Arab oil monopoly, the great inflation, made even the most conservative investments balloon tremendously. Then, too, he must have thought that his descendants would live by the standards he believed in. It's clear that they do not, but that's hindsight. And he wasn't really old when he died; only fifty-six."

"That young? Say, Giles, is there any chance that . . . ?"

"Not the slightest. He was walking toward the sitting room to join his wife when he had a sudden heart attack. As he grabbed for support, he knocked over a vase, a large, very expensive Delft vase, that was standing on a marble pedestal next to him. He was quite heavy, and had just eaten a huge meal. Because of van Broek's wealth, and to protect his own professional standing, the family doctor insisted on a post-mortem examination. It proved to be a massive heart attack. His arteries were badly clogged, he was a heavy smoker, highly overweight, and he did very little exercise."

"Could someone have hit him on the head with the vase?" Lila asked.

"It was definitely a heart attack, Lila, no question about that. There were no marks on him of any kind. The size and shape of the pieces of the vase were consistent with its falling that short distance. The cover of the vase was unbroken, resting on his foot. He was alive—his wife heard the noise and came running immediately—for several minutes after she saw him. No one was in sight. The children who were still living at home, Wilhelmina and Victoria, came down seconds later, and the doctor was there within fifteen minutes. Although Cornelius was still alive when the doctor came, he was unable to save him. Why are you so suspicious, Lila?"

"When a man that rich dies that young," Lila persisted, "you're an idiot, Giles, if you don't suspect somebody helped him along."

"Fifty-six may sound young to you and me, Lila, but it isn't really. This was 1942, remember, when the life expectancy was somewhat lower than it is now. You shouldn't be so distrustful. Most people are upright and honest."

"Honest and upright? Yeah? Can you imagine what the *thought* of that much dough does to ordinary people who used to be sane? Eighteen million? Let me tell you something, Giles. If you could fix it so I could get that money if all six of them died, you'd have to chain me to the wall, and even then . . ."

"Yes, I see your point, Lila, but I don't think . . . I'm sure one or two of them are fantasizing about—but if you come down to actually doing it, that's a different story."

"You really believe that, Giles, don't you? That's why I

arranged for you to sleep late; I knew you'd be up all night worrying about what you did wrong and how to correct it. That problem I solved, so put it out of your mind."

"You've got the answer, Lila?"

"The answer is, there's *nothing* you can do about it so stop worrying. Oliver and Isabel and I will keep an eye on the creeps; you put your mind to finding the hidden message."

"Thanks, Lila. I feel much better now that I know I can't stop one of my guests from killing another one of my guests. Is that supposed to be comforting?"

"Yep. If you were a woman, you'd understand. Relax and enjoy, as Confucius used to say."

"And why is it so important that I find the hidden message? I'm going to try, of course—I don't like an unsolved puzzle—but what does it matter if I do or I don't?"

Lila looked at him in amazement. "You don't see? You must be in *some* state. Isabel, you've got to make sure Giles gets plenty of 'R and R.'"

"I'm trying, Lila, but when he's in this mood, it's like pulling teeth."

"Yeah, I can see that. Look at his jaw. And the veins standing out on his temples. Do us all a favor, Isabel; ring Oliver and, if he hasn't left already, ask him to send up two double martinis, very dry, while I explain a few little details to Giles. Make that three, one for me, too. Four, if you want to join us."

"I only drink a little wine at meals, Lila," Giles protested.

"So who's stopping you? I told Oliver to bring some wine with the sandwiches; drink some wine, too."

"Are you trying to get me drunk, Lila?"

"Not *drunk* drunk, just *relaxed* drunk. But good and relaxed. Now we will have a Socratic dialogue; I'm Socrates and you're Dumdummides. Got it? Okay. Now why didn't Cornelius van Broek tell you the hidden message so when the rightful heir solved the crossword puzzles and decoded the hidden message, he could show you his solution and you could shake his hand and make him an eighteen-millionaire?"

"Huh? Would you mind repeating that? No, don't bother, I get the idea. Van Broek didn't *tell* me the message, or rather, he didn't tell Henry Winston's grandfather the message, because fifty years later, Arnold Winston might not be alive, so he would have to tell someone else, me, the message, and when you hear things you don't always hear what was said and after fifty years you don't always remember things perfectly accurately."

"So why didn't he write down the message?"

"Maybe he didn't trust Arnold Winston? If Winston knew the message, he could make a deal with one of the heirs and become nine million dollars richer very easily."

"Written messages can get lost, too. So what kind of message is it, Giles? What do you do if Albert Kruger announces on Friday night, right after he's solved the third crossword, that the hidden message is the third verse of the Fitzgerald translation of *The Rubáiyát*, so would you please give him the eighteen million in small bills?"

"It can't be like that. It has to be an action message, Lila, that directs you to do something which puts the money in your hand."

"Right. Now suppose one of the creeps, say Sondra Stempel, figured that out, too. Then on Saturday morning Richard looks very rosy and happy but Eileen looks strained and pained, like she's been up all night sweating over a hot crossword and failing. So we know Richard isn't jumping for joy because the earth moved for him and Eileen. If you were Sondra, what would you think?"

"I would assume he had found the hidden message."

"Now Richie comes to me and asks could he please have a limousine, one with a big trunk because there may be a lot of gold bricks in the buried chest. What do I do?"

"You'd have to give him the car. And go with him, too."

"Not me, Giles. You. With your fancy sword cane. The one I saw sticking out of my friend's back a few months ago. Because you might need it, Giles. Because right behind Richie's limousine is going to be Sondra Stempel in a taxi. And while Richie is trying to follow the directions, Sondra is figuring if she should try to persuade Richie to share the wealth before he gets his belly slit open, or to run him off the road after he does the heavy digging and in that way, keep all the loot."

"My first choice," Isabel said, "is Kruger."

"All of them will see it, Isabel. It could be a procession. Like a funeral, with the car lights on and going through red lights."

Giles winced. "Do you have to use such graphic metaphor?"

"Facts are facts, Giles. Now what do we do about it?"

Isabel shook her head. "I don't agree with your scenario."

"It's one possibility," Lila conceded. "What's more likely is that whoever solves the puzzle is going to look *not* happy, is not going to lock himself in his room, not do anything different. If he's smart enough to find the message, he's smart enough to figure out how to collect without getting killed."

"Exactly, Lila. So Richard will sneak out of the house on Friday night and go to the treasure trove and we'll find out about it next morning when Richard's expensive lawyer calls us and orders Giles to officially declare Richard the rightful heir."

"But what's wrong with that, Isabel?" Giles asked. "Isn't that fulfilling the terms of the will?"

"What's wrong," Lila said, "is that the other five creeps can figure the same thing. Starting Friday noon, when I give out the third puzzles, they'll be watching each other like hawks. One move by anyone toward leaving the house and there'll be a blitzkrieg on."

"You have a solution, I take it?"

"I already told you what to do."

"What Lila means," Isabel said, "is that she wants you to find the hidden message. Fast."

"I'll do my best, but how will that help? Even if I succeed?"

"On Friday, at supper—"

"No. I can't announce that I've found the message. There's no proof that what I find is right. If one of the heirs finds the same message, I don't have the right to give him the inheritance, even if I knew where it was. If our analysis is correct, the heir has to get the inheritance himself."

"You don't know where it is?" Lila asked. "Then how do you know it's eighteen million dollars' worth?"

"The bank's trust officer told me," Giles explained. "The actual assets are in the bank, of course. What I don't know is where the chest is buried that contains the validation of the heir."

"You mean," Isabel asked, "something like: 'Whosoever appears before thee wearing this amulet, is the rightful heir'?"

"Or signet ring or favorite spats. It could be anything."

"The trust officer won't tell you what it is?"

"He doesn't know. Nor does he know how he's supposed to identify the heir, but I'm sure van Broek has a simple, foolproof method."

Isabel thought for a moment. "You'll never convince the heirs you don't know the key to the inheritance. If you announce that you've found the hidden message, we'd have to barricade ourselves in our room and stay alert all night."

"Even then," Lila reminded, "you'd have to watch out for variations of the old Sherlock Holmes trick, where one of the creeps sets the house on fire, so that when you grab the secret message and dash out of the house, the arsonist can snatch it from you."

"I promise, Lila, if I find the message which, right now seems very improbable, I'll destroy all the papers. Other than that, what else can I do?"

"Drink your lunch, Giles, and concentrate on how to hide a message in a crossword. Leave it to Isabel and me to find a way to get us out of this fine mess you've gotten us into."

ACROSS

1 Small barrels
5 Stallion
10 Dutch cheese
14 Leave out
15 Agent of fermentation
16 Of old
17 Row; rank
18 Star (Pref.)
19 Small heating vessel
20 Trying experience
22 Admiral Horatio ____
24 Narrative poem
26 Roman 103
27 Choral composition
30 Shearwater birds
34 Egg (Pref.)
35 Leasing
37 Fifth month (Fr.)
38 Cow's sound
39 Spanish lord

40 Tenth month (Abbr.)
41 Wrong (Pref.)
42 Those that interwind
46 Definite article
47 Gland-like
49 Russian councils
51 Qualified
52 Retired (Latin abbr.)
53 Said
56 Having a blood deficiency
60 Mister (Ger.)
61 Pile of stones used as a
      landmark
65 Simpleton
66 Potpourri
67 Caper
68 Preposition
69 Map or diagram
70 Cup (Fr.)
71 Burden

DOWN

1 Japanese stringed
   instrument
2 Arabian chieftain
3 Donated (Scot.)
4 Road
5 Colorless variety of opal
6 Faeroe Islands whirlwinds
7 Pad for a woman's hair
8 Russian region (Abbr.)
9 Collegian in
   Buckinghamshire, Eng.
10 Optic covering
11 Specks
12 River of Italy
13 Intend
21 Three-banded armadillo
23 Inner Hebrides island
25 Novel by Voltaire (1759)
26 Of an E. Asian republic
27 Mark of punctuation
28 Keep away from

29 Hangman's halter
31 Show fear or hate, e.g.
32 Night (Ger.)
33 Locations
36 2,000 lbs. avoirdupois
42 Common infinitive (2
      words)
43 Lynx or eyra
44 Tale of chivalry
45 Scandinavian man's name
48 Native sodium carbonate
50 Angry
53 Store
54 Narrate
55 Operatic melody
57 One (Pref.)
58 Ninth Greek letter
59 Lump of clay
62 Collection of anecdotes
63 Possessive pronoun
64 Part of "to laugh" (Fr.)

Puzzle No. 2

16

"**T**HIS ONE WASN'T ANY HARDER THAN THE FIRST," LILA said. "But I still don't see a message."

"I don't know," Isabel said. "I had trouble with thirty Across and twenty-three Down. I had to look them up. I hate when two very obscure words cross on a nonobvious letter."

"There's no law against using reference books," Giles said.

"It's considered a sin by purists," Lila said, "but who has time for fancy religions? It's when you have to look it up a second time that you should be shunned. So, Giles, what do you see?"

"Nothing. Nothing at all. It's all blurry. Two double martinis and a glass of wine; that's more than I drink in a week."

"Go lie down on the couch, sissy. Isabel and I will mess this one up without your help. What do you see, Isabel?"

"Well, there are some more food words to add to the list from Puzzle Number One. 'KEGS,' 'HORSE'—in France it's common—'EDAM,' 'YEAST.' 'TIER' in German, is animal. 'HAGDENS'—I don't have the faintest idea if they're edible, probably not, but what the hell. 'OVO,' there was an egg in Number One, wasn't there? 'MOO,' close enough. 'FOOL,' that's an English dessert. 'OLIO,' that's like a stew. 'TASSE' as in 'demi-tasse.' 'RAT'? Yuch, but I guess if you're hungry enough... 'APAR,' same thing goes. 'WILDCAT.' Is that worse than 'RAT'?"

"You missed 'CHINESE,'" Lila said. "When I was a girl, it was always, 'Let's go eat Chinese.' But I don't see a pattern there. Hey, Giles, wasn't van Broek a big eater?"

"*Sh*, Lila. He's sleeping. I think we're better off with the geographic approach; there's plenty here. 'EDAM,' that's Holland, where van Broek was born. 'NELSON' is England;

London to be exact, where his column is. 'CIII' is Rome. 'DON' is Spain. 'SOVIETS.' 'HERR' is German. 'TASSE' is France. 'KOTO' is Japan. 'EMIR' is Arab. 'GIED' is Scotland. 'OES' is Faeroe Islands, that's near Iceland. 'SSR' is Russia again. 'ETONIAN,' of course. 'ARNO' is Italy. 'EIGG' is the Hebrides, Scotland again. 'CANDIDE,' France again. 'CHINESE.' 'NACHT' is German again. 'SVEN' is Scandinavian. 'IOTA,' Greece. And 'RIS' is France for the third time. Let's plot them on the map."

Isabel took the big atlas from the shelf and opened it to the Mercator projection. Lila quickly marked the points on the map. "What a mishmash. Or *olio*, if you'd rather. Nothing."

"Let's try putting the ones from Puzzle One on, too. Maybe if we connect the dots . . . ?"

Lila added the Puzzle One spots. "This is even worse. I don't see any sensible path. You want to try the connect-the-dots technique?" She lightly sketched in the lines. "God. If this is meant to be anything, it's beyond me."

"Could the dots be letters?" Isabel asked. "Like a dot-matrix printer makes? Maybe they'll show up if we add the third set of geographical clues?"

Lila took off her reading glasses and squinted at the map. "Nope. Nothing. You could add ten sets of dots and it would still be nothing. Let's try the first letters of the geographic words. Read them off to me."

"H-L-R-S-S-G-F-J—"

"Stop. Forget it. I don't think it's worth it. It didn't work for Puzzle One, but let's try the diagonals. 'KMEEPT-NOEOEEOTD.' Now let's waste our time on the other one, left to right. 'PLRTBIIOIAILTRM.' Crap."

"How about Stepquotes?"

"I already looked. Zilch."

"The middle square? The outer square? The diagonal square?"

"One word pops out: "THE,' from the middle of the right side reading down to the left. Otherwise, it's dead. I'm beginning to think we really have to wait for Puzzle Number Three. Remember what Giles said, that van Broek was a very square conservative type. If he said we had to write down all the words before the key pops out, we better figure on writing *all* the words, not two-thirds of them."

"Are you giving up already, Lila? That's not like you."

"It sure as hell is like me, Isabel. If I don't get it right away, I don't get it at all. Let's concentrate on what I promised Giles: that we'd figure out what to do when, if, one of the creeps found the message. You got anything?"

"Well, we could all follow him and protect him from the others."

"I should risk my life to protect Gloria Raffa? Are you kidding?"

"How about hiring a detective agency to station a couple of men front and back, to follow whoever sneaks out of the house after Friday, to protect him from whoever follows him?"

"Suppose Kruger takes off ten o'clock Friday night. Our guys watch him. Then five minutes later, Eileen sneaks out. They shoot her or handcuff her. Later she proves that she found the message and was prevented from beating Kruger to the treasure by our thugs. *Forcibly*. And to top it off, Kruger was just sneaking out to buy some cigars." Lila stared at Isabel over her glitter-covered glasses.

"What did you have in mind, Lila? When you wanted Giles to find the secret message?"

"Giles finds the message; he's good at stuff like that. Look what he did in the Brundage case. We station somebody near the buried treasure, but out of sight—behind a tree, say, I don't want to give Victoria heart failure—with a camera. And a strong flash. He takes a picture of her digging up the ironbound treasure chest and we have proof she won legitimately."

"But you said before—one of the others will follow her, kill her, and steal the treasure. What does our guy do then?"

"Takes a picture of that, too."

"He doesn't try to stop her? The murderer?"

"From showing the kind of initiative that Cornelius van Broek had? Wasn't old Cornelius one of the robber barons? He should be proud that the line breeds true."

"But *murder*? We've got to stop it, Lila."

"Honey, when somebody wants to kill somebody, *really* wants to, eighteen-million-dollar wants to, somebody else can't stop it. He can just watch. And take movies."

"No, Lila, we can't just let somebody get killed. Our guard has to stop the murderer."

"Okay, Isabel. If that situation arises, we'll hire an armed guard and pray that he shoots the right guy. And"—she added as an afterthought—"that he shoots first."

17

"**H**OW CAN IT BE GOOD," GILES ASKED, "TO HAVE DINNER with the heirs, if it's bad to have lunch with them?"

"Supper," Lila said, "what you rich millionaires call dinner, is a more formal-type occasion than lunch, so you can put the creeps in their places. A tux, Oliver?"

"Exactly, Mrs. Quinn. To dominate without threatening."

"I didn't bring an evening gown," Isabel said. "I was under the impression this was going to be a vacation."

"So wear a plain black cocktail, Isabel, with pearls. On you it'll look like a million."

"Why do I have to domineer, Lila? These are guests in my house."

"These *guests*, Giles, are busy figuring how to screw each other out of eighteen million. To accomplish that, they have to get past you first. So they've been working on you, trying to make you feel that you're screwing *them* out of their rights and their inheritance."

"You think they've combined against me, Lila? That's ridiculous."

"Not combined like they've signed a pact in blood; they each came to the same conclusion independently. They're trying to throw you off balance so you'll be more worried about how you're treating them rather than if they're living up to the rules of the game."

"And you think that appearing at the dinner table in a tux will do the trick?"

"Every little bit helps, Giles. It took me two minutes to give out Puzzle Number Two today. You know why? I just told them what to do or else, and they did it. No nonsense, not like yesterday. Now you're going down there and sit at the head of the table, the lord of the manor. You'll make them feel like peasants, clumsy, dirty, underdressed peas-

nts. Pissants. And if they start anything, Isabel and I will
traighten them out, but quick."

"We could have done that at breakfast and lunch, too,
Lila. I really wanted to study them. Just in case."

"Breakfast and lunch are less formal. This way, it looks
ke you're getting breakfast in bed and can't stand the sight
f them at lunch. It's only your sense of *noblesse oblige* that
orces you to grace their dinner with your presence. As far
s judging their characters, forget it. All bets are off when
hey're racing for the gold."

Oliver coughed discreetly. "I believe I can offer some
nformation that might be of use, sir. The staff is quite mind-
ul of your interests."

"You recruited them as spies, Oliver? So much per report?"

"I have impressed on the staff the value of being obser-
ant. And of reporting to me any unusual occurrences. There
re some small bonuses, of course, proportional to the value
f the information obtained. I have found that an appeal to
he sense of duty, coupled with some concrete evidence of
ur appreciation, produces the best results."

"And what results have we produced, Oliver?"

"Victoria van Broek is not quite the sweet old lady she
ould like us to think she is. She seems to be highly in favor
f slavery as a working relationship. Carmen requested per-
ission to slug her."

"Which you did not grant, I take it?"

"Carmen is a big woman, sir. I did not wish Miss van
Broek removed from the lists by a valued staff member; it
ould be too hard to replace Carmen. I merely pointed out
o Miss van Broek that it does not make sense to antagonize
 person who is in a position to, shall we say, spit in the
oup? And that good domestics are in very short supply and
ommand net bankable remuneration considerably in excess
f that earned by midlevel executives. Miss van Broek, hav-
g once known wealth, has great respect for those who live
life free from financial cares, even if they are in service."

"How much does Carmen get?" Lila asked.

"You must realize, Mrs. Quinn, that Carmen will be taking
are of all the needs of three people and an entire floor for
fteen hours a day for seven consecutive days, plus two
ays of preparation and one day of demobilization afterward.
eople who are unaccustomed to having servants can be

very demanding. With all respect, Mrs. Quinn, you coul
not perform at maximum efficiency under those conditions.

"My muscles or my mouth, Oliver?"

"I'm afraid, Mrs. Quinn, that domestic service is not fo
ladies of a certain age who are unable to conceal an otherwis
praiseworthy independence of spirit."

"I wouldn't last five minutes, is that it, Oliver?"

"I'm afraid you would find yourself explaining forcefull
to Miss Ashe that one does not leave a room looking like
college dormitory. Or telling Mr. Deddich he is not bein
helpful when he makes his own bed, for instance, since
would not pass my inspection and you would have to tak
it apart before you made the bed properly."

"Any dirt? Useful dirt?"

"I'm afraid not, Miss Isabel, at least not yet. Agnes report
that Mr. Kruger tried to pinch her, that Miss Stempel is nc
only—I must quote—'a filthy slob', but that she also brough
with her a highly provocative lacy black nightgown, and tha
Miss Raffa evidently stayed up all night working and drinkin
straight vodka."

"You never know what's useful, Oliver," Giles said. "Kee
up the good work and let me know of anything unusual a
once."

"Thank you, sir, one does one's best. May I suggest w
start dressing for dinner soon, sir? Your clothes are laid ou
If you wish, Mrs. Quinn, Gina will help you set your hai
she is quite skilled at that."

"Are you trying to tell me politely, Oliver, that I shoul
do something with my hair? I have news for you; nothin
will help my hair, but I'd like to let her try. I'll be in m
room in five minutes. You're sure she can spare the time?

"The second floor is much easier to take care of than th
third and fourth floors, Mrs. Quinn. Gina will be with yo
shortly."

Lila turned to Giles. "One more thing, Giles. I've bee
thinking. Maybe it would be better if you didn't say anythin
at dinner tonight. Let Isabel and me do all the talking. Ju
look preoccupied, like you have more important things
think about than your creepy guests."

"But that's not—It's impolite. I'm the host. Why . . . ?"

"Because, Giles—look, I hate to insult you to your face
but the trouble with you is that you're a gentleman. Yo

can't help treating creeps and bums as if they lived up to the same standards you do. To you, every woman is a lady and every man a gentleman until proven different. The trouble is, proving different usually means some good guy gets his head banged in by the testee, who then pleads environment. I don't make a fuss, that's how life works today: the bad guys usually win and the good guys usually lose. But I'm directly involved here; not just me, but you and Isabel and Oliver, too. I don't want my head banged in, and I don't want yours banged in either. So I'm telling you, Giles, unless you're ready to treat these *momzers* the way they should be treated, stay out of my way. Let me handle them, me and Isabel. I'm no gentleman, thank God, and neither is Isabel. And luckily for you, I'm no lady either, so what Isabel can't do, I can. Okay?" She opened the study door. "Now I'm going to get my hair fixed. It never hurts to *look* like a lady. Camouflage."

18

"**S**O NICE TO SEE YOU, MR. SULLIVAN," VICTORIA VAN Broek said. "We missed you at breakfast and lunch."

"Mr. Sullivan is very busy," Lila said, "but as host, he felt obligated to join you at dinner."

There was silence as the avocado stuffed with crabmeat was served, and even greater silence while it was eaten. As Hazel cleared the bowls away, Richard said, "You seem upset about something, Mrs. Quinn. I hope it's nothing that concerns me."

The clear chicken consommé was served. Lila sipped a spoonful and decided to be, for her, reasonably polite. "You six are so intent on the carrot dangling in front of your noses that you forget where you are. Mr. Sullivan has graciously invited you into his home. You're all living in a way you never dreamed of. Instead of living up to your surroundings, you squabble and backbite and make life miserable for your host and his other guests."

"You have a point, Mrs. Quinn," Victoria agreed. "We have been behaving rather badly." She looked at Giles contritely. "I do apologize, Mr. Sullivan, for all of us, particularly Gloria and Sondra." Gloria shot her a killing look, but said nothing. Sondra grasped her knife white-knuckle hard, then put it down and went on eating. "But you are wrong," Victoria continued, "about one thing, Mrs. Quinn. This kind of life may be new to you, but I lived this way, with even more servants—mine alone, not shared with two others—for the first twenty-two years of my life. And even more servants for the next seven years, until my dear husband passed away."

"Just to clarify things," Gloria Raffa said, equally sweetly, "passed away is not the most accurate way to describe jumping off a penthouse balcony, but I guess when your life is made so miserable that—"

"Carl was not miserable. He loved me, and he did not jump." Victoria spat out the last words. "It was an accident, the police said; he'd been drinking."

"When your name is van Broek, the police will kiss—"

"See what I mean?" Lila broke in. "Animals. You can dress them up to make them look human, but wave a lamb chop in front of their faces and the fangs come out."

"I resent that, Mrs. Quinn," Richard said quietly. "I have behaved like a perfect gentleman every moment I've been a guest here, exactly as, I'm sure, great-grandfather Cornelius would have behaved, and a lot better than my dear relatives."

"Oh, Richard," Eileen smiled, "you're such a transparent amateur. Do you really think you can fool Mrs. Quinn?"

"He can't, cutie-pie, and neither can you," Lila said. "Acting doesn't count in your favor very much, even good acting. In fact, when I catch you acting, and I've caught each one of you at least once, I take off points."

Oliver served the roast chicken with tarragon, with braised white onions and sautéed browned parsnips. All talk stopped, in appreciation of Ping's artistry. As she was getting seconds of everything, Sondra addressed Lila Quinn. "Do you think it's good manners to keep on insulting us? Or, as a judge, trying to provoke us into behavior that will eliminate us from the contest?"

Lila smiled widely. "Nope, it's not good behavior, dearie, but I wasn't hired for my manners. I'm supposed to judge which one of you inherits eighteen million, in case nobody solves the puzzle. I can test you any way I like, and you have to take it. Even knowing this, I'll bet at least one of you is going to be eliminated for conduct unbecoming a van Broek."

"My father never lost his temper, Mrs. Quinn." Victoria also smiled. "But anyone who crossed him ended up very badly. Very badly indeed. That's a *real* van Broek trait, Mrs. Quinn. We all have van Broek blood in our veins, and I have the most."

"Threats also count against you, honey."

"Threats? Nonsense, Mrs. Quinn. I was merely giving you firsthand information about family characteristics. Something you might not have known about."

"I didn't know about it, Vickie dear, but I sort of deduced

that van Broeks weren't made of spun sugar and angelica."

Watercress salad was served. "What's for dessert?" Kruger asked. "I don't want to waste my calories on grass."

"Force yourself, Al," Gloria said, "there's lots of garlic in the dressing."

"Well, in that case..." Kruger filled his bowl with salad and poured on a lot of the dressing. He took a big chunk of the hot crusty bread.

"You're digging your grave with your teeth, Albert," Victoria said. "Daddy died of overeating at just your age."

"He was fifty-six, Auntie; I'm forty-eight. And he died of a heart attack."

"From overeating, my dear nephew, but go right ahead, if you insist. At your age, you look exactly the way Daddy looked when he died, the night he died. If we're lucky, it might be tonight for you, too."

Albert stopped eating and put his hand to his chest. His face was tense.

"You feel the symptoms already, dear nephew?" Victoria asked, over-solicitously.

"Just a touch of indigestion," Kruger said, and began eating again. "Tough luck, Auntie."

The tension around the table relaxed a bit. "I don't mind your needling us, Mrs. Quinn," Gloria said. "I can take care of myself. But to take off points for trouble that you stirred up yourself is not only lousy, it's entrapment, and if you try it on me, *dearie*, you're letting yourself in for real trouble."

"Setting up fake causes for a possible lawsuit when you lose, costs a lot of points, kiddo, especially when you're the one who urged Kruger to eat more, even though he's fifty pounds overweight right now. I also find it very interesting that you're no longer so sure you're going to win."

"Mr. Sullivan"—Eileen tried to catch Giles's eyes—"do you think it's right for Mrs. Quinn to keep trying, to provoke me into acting out so she can eliminate me?"

Before Giles could respond, Lila spoke up. "Don't bother Mr. Sullivan, kid; ask me. I make the rules around here, unless there's something in the will that says I'm wrong. There isn't. If you can't take the heat, get out of the kitchen."

"The heat is unnecessary, Mrs. Quinn," Eileen said. "We have a hard enough job to do as it is."

"Trouble solving the crosswords? I offered a refresher course; everyone turned it down."

"The crosswords are easy; it's the message that's hard."

"Gee, and I always thought that people got paid eighteen million a week just for breathing. What did you expect, girlie? If it was easy, all six of you would be hitting each other with shovels instead of digging."

"And that's another thing, Mrs. Quinn. Your constant harping on character, inherited characteristics. As I read the will, the first person to decode the secret message inherits everything. Character has nothing to do with it."

"You're absolutely right, Eileen. So if you're sure, absolutely sure, you're going to be the winner that way, go ahead, be your usual nasty self. But if you're not absolutely sure..."

Dessert was chocolate soufflé. Isabel finished first and looked up at Oliver. He had another portion ready. Everyone took seconds, and sat back stuffed. Isabel took thirds. When she had finished, Giles stood up. The rest followed suit. Albert Kruger had to put his weight on the table to get up. Oliver moved beside him. "Are you all right, sir?"

"My right hip; the bursitis. It's getting worse."

"Would you like some aspirin, sir?"

"I've already taken Naprosyn and aspirin. I'll be all right, thank you."

"Perhaps a cane, sir?"

"Yes. Good idea, Oliver." Kruger turned to Giles. "Do you have a cane I could borrow, Mr. Sullivan?"

Giles glared at Oliver. "I'm sorry, Mr. Kruger, but the only one I have is this one, which I must always carry. Tomorrow morning—the stores are closed now—Oliver will get you a cane. And anything else you might need."

"Please feel free to use the elevator for down trips, too, sir," Oliver said.

"Once I get the cane, I'll be all right. I don't intend to leave my room tonight anyway."

"Good idea, Kruger," Lila said. "Industriousness, that's the ticket. See you at noon tomorrow, kids. Puzzle Number Three."

19

ISABEL CAREFULLY OPENED THE DOOR OF THE STUDY AND stuck her head in. "All gone?"

"The coast is clear," Lila said.

"How were they?"

"Like pussycats. One touch of the lash was all they needed, and they remembered from last night."

"I'm still not sure," Giles objected, "that guests—they are my guests, Lila, no matter what you say—that guests should be subjected to such bullying."

"Better them than you, Giles," Lila said. "The only question is, how long will they stay that way? I'm sure that right now, all six of them are wasting valuable time figuring how to get rid of me."

"Oh, no, Lila"—Isabel put her hand to her mouth. "You put yourself in danger just to—"

"You've got murder on your mind, Isabel. Probably because you're the type that, if anybody had talked to you the way I did to them last night, his lifeless body would be found at the foot of the cliff the next morning. No, that's not it. They're busy looking for a way to make Giles remove me as judge of the contest and to substitute somebody easier to con."

"Nonsense, Lila; I would never remove you. Even if I did, who else could I get that would suit their requirements."

"You, dear," Isabel said.

"Me? I'm easier to con? I was a criminal lawyer for thirty-five years, and I've met the worst . . ."

"Yes, dear, but they're the ones who got caught. These—what was the term you used, Lila?"

"*Momzers.* Should really be *mamzerim*, for the plural, like cherub*im* and seraph*im*, but we usually Anglicize it to *momzers*. Means bastards. It can also be used affectionately, especially if the grandchildren pull a fast one on you. If? No 'if' about it. *When.*"

"Yes, Giles, exactly. *Momzers.* These *momzers* are not like ordinary murderers who get caught. They'll find a way to skin you alive so that you'll thank them for it."

"Is it true," Lila asked, "what Gloria Raffa said? That Victoria's husband committed suicide?"

Giles hesitated. "The police called it an accident, and it was hushed up very quickly."

"But . . . ?" Lila prompted.

"The penthouse railing was almost four feet high. It's very hard to fall over something like that accidentally, even if you've had several drinks."

"He was drunk?" Isabel asked.

"No, the autopsy showed only mild— Three or four martinis, at most."

"But why? Was Victoria really as bad as Gloria said?"

"No, not at all. They'd been married only a few years, seven or eight, and seemed to lead a life full of pleasure. What I found out later . . . they had run out of money, that was the trouble. They were deeply in debt, and Carl couldn't take it."

"Couldn't they go to her family? And what about her inheritance?"

"They spent without thinking. Victoria is smart, very smart, but she was never very sensible. As for her family, you've seen an example of how much family feeling there is in that family. Even her mother . . . they were against the marriage from the start."

"So that's why Victoria's so poor."

"She's been living off the income of what was left of Carl's insurance after the debts were paid." He explained to Lila. "Old Cornelius was very strict. He ran his family the way he ran his company. He gave orders and you followed them. Precisely. No deviation. I'm sure Victoria—she was twenty-one when she met Carl Locherwald—a grown woman . . . She could not marry without her father's consent. There is so much, Lila, that you don't know about the van Broek family, some really tragic . . . I think it would be better if I told you about—"

"Forget it, Giles; the last thing those *momzers* need is sympathy and understanding. And they're not going to get it from me, no matter what a hard life they had. I had a hard life, too, and so did you, when you were a kid."

"Lila's right, Giles," Isabel said. "Let's keep it this way: Lila handles the contest and you handle me."

"You seem to be in a particularly good mood this morning, Isabel. What happened?"

"Oliver got a big delivery this morning. Mostly Dutch."

"Ah, I wondered why you got up so early today."

"Doctor's orders. For my nerves."

"Now that you have a confidence-inducing hoard of your miracle drug, can we get down to business?"

Lila handed them each a copy of the third puzzle.

ACROSS

1 Horse's mouth congestion
7 Strike and rebound
12 Lead in
13 Nonprofessional
16 One who buys cheap and
    sells at a profit
    (Colloq.)
17 Enzyme found in yeast
18 Benign cyst
19 Lay at rest
21 Pouch
22 Cuckoo birds
24 Smiles radiantly
25 Extraordinarily big
26 Son of Abraham and
    Sarah
28 Chain or rope (Naut.)
29 Temptations
30 Wise old men
32 Female celebrity
34 Bantu language
35 Food scrap

36 Fighting
40 Full of rage
44 Foreign; strange
45 Long, narrow arm of the
    sea
47 Between (Fr.)
48 Mischievous children
49 Herb used in cookery
51 Unit of metric weight
52 Be soaking wet
53 ___ de Balzac
54 Hydrocarbon (Suff.)
55 Medical school cofounded
    (1838) by O. W.
    Holmes
57 1833 novel, " ___Grandet"
60 Province of Albania
61 Odors
62 Maugham's Miss
    Thompson
63 Indian drum (Hyph.)

DOWN

1 Formal authorization
2 Liar
3 Roman 1,550
4 Young seal
5 Harsh; austere
6 Paved ways
7 Mercurous chloride used
    as a purgative
8 Accumulate
9 Speed contest
10 Baseball player, Mel ___
11 Ascertain the dimensions
14 Employments
15 Alcove; niche
16 Country gallant
20 Compensate
23 Derisive literature
25 The chase
27 Common quail
29 Motion-picture actor,
    Peter ___

31 Stood as a candidate
33 Acknowledgment of debt
36 Central parts
37 Himalayan district
38 Tools for tearing
39 One to whom an accession
    is made (Law)
40 Most impartial
41 Walpole novel, The Castle
    of ___
42 Homosexuality
43 Strewn with a pattern
    (Her.)
46 Equal (Pref.)
49 Actress, Beulah ___
50 White (Pref.)
53 C. American nation
    (Abbr.)
56 Sound from a lamb or kid
58 Precious stone
59 Adjective suffix

Puzzle No. 3

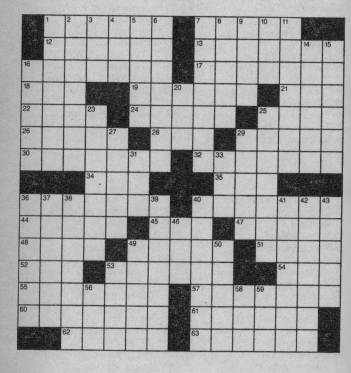

"**T**HERE'S DEFINITELY A MESSAGE IN THIS ONE," ISABEL said. "No one kills all four corners just for fun. Remember what we found in Washington?"

"Washington?" Lila asked.

"We found some unusual puzzles there," Giles said hurriedly, "this summer, when we were on vacation. They were published in *The Capitol Gazette*."

"You went to Washington on vacation in the *summer*?"

"It was the only time Isabel could get away." Isabel put her foot down on his, hard. "For the Fourth of July celebration. Very exciting. Isabel got a big bang out of it."

"Puzzle Number One"—Isabel changed the subject—"had two corners blocked out, but that was only one box, and it was upper right and lower left. This one has two boxes blocked, including upper left."

"Yeah, and when you compare the patterns of the three puzzles," Lila said, "they're so different, I don't believe they all contain the same message. It has to be a continuous message."

"Or a combined message," Giles said, "where you need all three parts fitted together to make sense."

"Anyway," Isabel said, "it's probably a fairly long message, so that's a help."

"It would be a help," Giles said, "if it were a long message, but it could be the type where Puzzle One gives the instructions as to how to apply Puzzle Two, the key, to Puzzle Three, which contains the actual message."

"If that's it," Lila said, "we're sunk. To solve that kind of setup would take a full black room."

"Couldn't we hire some cryptographers, Giles? As consultants? Some of your old acquaintances from Washington, perhaps?"

"I don't think it would be appropriate, Isabel. This is, after all, a private matter that we should handle ourselves."

"But we've done all three puzzles, Giles, written all the words down, followed the instructions, and I still don't see a single lead. Do you see anything?"

"No, Isabel, every pattern I've tried doesn't seem to produce even the possibility of a message. No Stepquotes, no diagonals, no squares, no diamonds, nothing."

"There's very little on food either," Lila said, "or geography. I don't see any consistent pattern at all."

"How about going back to a Cardano Grille, Giles? See if any combination of words, in order, makes a message."

All three bent over their filled-out puzzles. After several minutes, Lila said, "If anyone can find a message in 'LAMPAS, CAROM, INDUCT, AMATEUR, SCALPER, LACTASE, WEN, REPOSE, SAC, ANIS, BEAMS, and HUGE,' he's a better man than I am, Gunga Din. And if you want to start from the bottom up, help yourself."

"Maybe it's first letters only." Isabel began writing. "'L, C, I, A, S, L, W, R, S, A, B, H.'" She stopped. "Nothing. Does that look like a code of any kind to you, Giles?"

"If it is a code, Isabel, it isn't a very obvious one. Let me try last letters. 'S, M, T, R, R, E, N, E, C, S, S, E.' That doesn't look any better either. What do you think, Lila?"

"While you were doing that, I was trying the bottom half of the puzzle. We're shooting blanks, Giles."

"I can't believe it's that difficult," Isabel said. "You told me that Cornelius van Broek was a simple, straightforward man. Is it likely that he would hide the message so deeply, so complexly, that the three of us can't find it?"

"You must be patient, Isabel. In solving codes, you can spend a very long time pounding your head against a wall, then all of a sudden you get a flash of insight and everything falls apart."

"What troubles me," Lila said, "is that this doesn't seem to suit Cornelius van Broek's character as you described him to me. I think we're making our job harder unnecessarily."

"What do you mean, Lila?"

"We're looking for something that isn't there. Stepquotes, for instance. They didn't exist when this puzzle was constructed."

"Cornelius could have stumbled on the technique accidentally."

"Anything is possible, Giles, but I'll play the odds. The message has to be hidden in plain sight in a very simple way. What we have to do is think like Cornelius van Broek."

"Fine," Isabel enthused. "I'm in just the mood. Let's decorticate Sullivan, for beginners."

"What's come over you, Isabel? A short time ago you were in such a good mood."

"I was drugged. Now I see myself wasting my whole vacation pounding my head against a wall, hoping to get a flash of insight. And when I get back to Windham, there'll be another wall or two waiting on my desk. Or three."

"The two of you," Lila ordered, "get out of here. You're disturbing my peace. If I have to think simple, I need quiet, tranquility. Lambs gamboling and shepherds playing wooden flutes."

"Sorry," Isabel apologized. "Sometimes it gets to be too much. In school, I'm so efficient, everyone envies me. Here ...? Everything I try to do, for Giles as well as for myself, everything turns sour."

"Go bite some Belgian chocolates for a change, kid; more fat. Builds up the myelin sheath around your nerves. Go take a break; I'll solve this puzzle for you."

"Do you really think so, Lila? I'm so frustrated."

"Sure. Guaranteed. Look, old Cornelius didn't want the problem *unsolved*, he wanted it solved, wanted one of his descendants to win. That's why he left all that money to him. Her. He just wanted to make it hard enough so that only one of them won, that's all. So if one of those *momzers* can do it, you think Lila Quinn can't?"

"Sure, Lila," Isabel said. "If one of them can do it, you can do it, too. Faster." She took Giles's arm, apologetically, and led him to the door. Then she looked back at Lila. "But what if one of them can't do it?"

"Pray that one of them can," Lila said grimly. "Because if *none* of them can, you better get ready to find five bodies floating face down in the swimming pool."

"Swimming pool?" Giles sounded dazed.

"Or lifeless bodies found crushed at the foot of the cliff," Lila said impatiently.

"What cliff? I still don't understand."

"Figure of speech, Giles," Lila said patiently. She waved her fingers in front of his eyes. He didn't even blink. "You've got to stop concentrating, Giles; get your mind off these lousy puzzles and do something relaxing. I may need a simple mind to bounce ideas off, later. Go away. I don't want to see you until suppertime. Excuse me, dinner. On second thought, who needs you for dinner? You cramp my style."

"You seemed to do rather well last night, Lila, even with me present."

"That? Wouldn't faze a five-year-old where I come from. Yeah, the more I think of it, the better I like it. I'll tell Oliver to set up dinner, you and Isabel, in your room tonight. I don't want to see you until breakfast tomorrow, here in the study. Unless you get the sudden flash of revelation, in which case, call me at once. Isabel, can you think of something to do with him until tomorrow? Something mindless? Relaxing?"

"I'll try," Isabel said.

21

THE PHONE WOKE GILES AT SEVEN O'CLOCK. IT WAS Oliver. "I'm sorry to disturb you, sir, but I must see you at once, on the third floor. Just a dressing gown will do. Don't wake Miss Isabel. Please use the elevator." Oliver hung up.

"Who is it?" Isabel murmured, half asleep.

"I have to see Oliver for a moment, dear; go back to sleep." Giles moved quickly, alarmed. Oliver did not ask for help lightly.

Albert Kruger lay at the bottom of the stairs, his head on the third-floor landing, twisted at a very bad angle. To his left lay the new cane which, clearly, had not helped. Agnes, the third-floor maid, was standing stiffly, hands clasped in front of her, out of sight of the body. "Dead?" Giles asked.

"For several hours, sir," Oliver said. "Before midnight, I would judge. I made my last round at ten-fifteen. Agnes found Mr. Kruger and called me at once."

"You've taken precautions?"

"Yes, sir. Our guests were phoned by the floor maids and told to stay in their rooms with the doors locked. Individual breakfasts would be served at eight by Carmen and Agnes, and on your floor, by Gina."

"Isabel?"

"When Miss Macintosh opens the bedroom door, she will be informed by Gina."

"Foul play?"

"No sign of it, sir, but I made only a superficial examination."

"Papers? Other useful clues?"

"A pocket handkerchief and a pencil."

"Newspapers? TV?"

"The night man is staying on duty at the front door until I relieve him. He has lots of strong coffee. I assigned the footman to the ground-floor service entrance."

"The police?"

"It would be advisable, sir, but I wished to discuss the matter with you first."

"I see no alternative, Oliver. The legal ramifications..."

"Precisely, sir. If you were to call Mr. Percival?"

"He will be very nasty, Oliver. The least I can expect will be a long, embarrassing lecture."

"I'm sure he will be most understanding, sir. You might remind him that Lieutenant Faber was most helpful in the Brundage affair."

Giles squared his shoulders.

"Another one?" Percival exploded. His normal chief-of-detectives voice had not softened since his formal retirement. "In your own house? Again? That's *two*, Giles, in less than a year."

"I know, Percival; I can count."

"Are you trying to make me look bad, Giles? Because if you are..."

"No, Percival, I did not order a murder to embarrass you or to besmirch the name of Sullivan. This has nothing to do with you."

"The hell it doesn't. Anything any Sullivan does has to do with me, and especially my own brother. The boys don't ever let me forget how many killers are walking the streets right now, thanks to you. And especially that one of them killed a cop after."

"I'm really sorry about that, Percival, you know I am, but my duty is to my client. I had no way of knowing that..."

"Four kids he had, Giles. Four kids. Orphans. And a widow."

"Nothing I say now can help, Percival. I did retire right afterward, and I did set up a scholarship fund."

"Blood money, Giles. Cop's blood."

"Would you want a man to go on trial without a lawyer? They do that in some countries, you know; sentence first, trial after."

"But it don't have to be you who does it, Giles, or anybody as good as you. Leave it to Legal Aid; they put enough killers back on the street as it is. It don't have to be a Sullivan."

Giles sighed. "All right, Percival. Sorry I bothered you. Good-bye." He started to hang up the phone.

"Wait," Percival shouted. "What are you so damn touchy for? I didn't say I wouldn't help. What do you want?"

"Advice. Help. Thanks, Percival."

"Don't thank me, Giles; I'm doing it for Pop. He told me to take care of you."

"He also told me to take care of you and Mother, Perce. I guess we both have to take care of each other."

"I don't need you to take care of me. Did you call the station house yet?"

"You're the first one."

"Well, now you're beginning to show a little brains. Who smartened you up the past year, Oliver or Macintosh?"

"Oliver. Isabel is still sleeping."

"Still? You got her into this, too? A second time? What the hell's the matter with you, Giles? A lady like that."

"It was an accident, Perce. Look, I'll explain everything later."

"Okay. I'll call it in. Don't touch anything, don't say anything, and don't do anything until I get there. Now get off the phone."

Giles hung up, feeling like a feather in a hurricane. A small, weak feather, with no control.

22

"THAT'S EVERYTHING, MR. SULLIVAN?" LIEUTENANT
Faber asked.

"I told him to level with you," Percival answered.

"With all due respect, Chief," Faber said politely, "I'd
like to hear him say it."

Percival nodded. "Fair enough, Lieutenant. But you know
me, and Giles knows me even better. My word is his word."

"The Lieutenant is right, Percival," Giles said, and
addressed Faber. "I told you everything I know. I'd like to
keep it out of the newspapers as long as possible."

"I could treat the house, the whole house, as a 'scene of
the crime,' Mr. Sullivan. That would keep out everybody
who didn't have to be there. Station a man front and back.
How're you fixed for food?"

"We have a well-stocked pantry and freezer, so that's no
problem. But we're still living here, all of us. What about
that?"

"Until the technical boys are finished, nobody uses the
stairs or the areas near the stairs."

"I've already arranged that. Only Oliver is on the floor
and he knows what not to do. The guests stay in their own
rooms."

"Okay, keep it that way until I talk to them. I don't want
them talking to each other until I get their statements."

"Can you keep the information about the contest out of
the papers until it's over? Wednesday noon? The TV report-
ers would have a field day with a story this unusual."

"What am I going to put in my report," Faber asked,
"about why those six were in your house? Especially
Kruger?"

"Leave it general, Lieutenant," Percival suggested. "Say
it had to do with a will, but no details."

"I could do that for a day, Chief, maybe two, but after that . . ."

"Mrs. Kruger." Giles was drained. "She'll talk."

"I could keep her tied up today," Faber volunteered, "maybe part of tomorrow, too, but that's it."

"Stall it as long as you can, Faber; you got to, if you want a chance to break the case. Breaking that other case my brother was involved in didn't look too bad on your record now, did it?"

"Yeah, I appreciated that. Okay, Chief, I'll do what I can."

"It may have been an accident," Giles offered.

"Yeah, I thought of that," Faber said. "Are the stairs always that badly lit?"

"Oh, no, Lieutenant. The small light in the middle of the stair is always on for safety, but if someone wants to walk down, he switches on the big light. It's right on the wall, to your right, at the landing. It stays on for one minute."

"To your right, going down, you mean?"

"Yes, exactly, and there's one to your left, going up."

"So before you start going down, you have a good light on the stairs? And the carpet was tight, no wrinkles? Do you really think it was an accident, Mr. Sullivan?"

"Well, he was overweight, and he had bursitis in his hip. It certainly could have been an accident. Or maybe it was a heart attack. He was a prime candidate, you know: fat, a smoker, no exercise. Type A personality."

"Yeah, sure. You want to go convince his wife of that?" Giles shook his head. "Neither do I, Mr. Sullivan, but I got to do it. You think she'll believe me? Eighteen million bucks? Hell, for that kind of dough, I'd push my mother-in-law down the stairs. For eighteen *thousand*."

"When will you have the medical examiner's report?" Giles asked.

"Why? You think there's a chance Kruger *wasn't* given a little help getting down the stairs fast?"

"I'm hoping, that's all, Lieutenant. It would complicate matters tremendously if he were pushed."

"You think the M.E. can tell if he was pushed or not? How? From the fingerprints on his bathrobe, or from *no* fingerprints on his bathrobe?"

"If he had a heart attack, wouldn't that show?"

"A heart attack doesn't take two seconds, Mr. Sullivan.

Even if the M.E. finds a clot obstructing a coronary artery, that doesn't mean Kruger *wasn't* pushed. And the cause of death would still be the push that broke his neck; lots of people live after heart attacks."

"Yes, I know, but the pain of a heart attack, a sudden great pain like that, that grips the chest, it could make him lose his balance, drop his cane, fall down the stairs."

"It could, Mr. Sullivan. Also, it couldn't. Some heart attacks, 'silent' heart attacks, are painless and have practically no symptoms."

"He's right, Giles," Percival said. "It's like the one Pop had. In his sleep, thank God. What are you getting at, Giles? If Kruger's foot slipped, how can the M.E. tell? If he had a chest pain, maybe it caused him to fall down the stairs, but how can the doc say for sure? You want a 'death by accidental means'? Or a 'natural causes'? How does that help you?"

"Then I can go on with the legacy contest and, after it's over, forget about the whole thing."

"From what you told me about Mrs. Kruger," Faber said, "I don't think she's going to accept that. I don't know how she felt about her husband, but everybody loves eighteen million bucks. The way you described the contest, if an heir ain't around, he can't win. Do I have it right?"

"Well, yes, that's the way it works."

"So Mrs. Kruger's only chance to get the eighteen million, or any part of it, is to claim that the winner, whoever's going to be the winner, killed her husband. I think she's got a pretty good case, don't you, counsellor?"

"Not if the medical examiner finds he died of natural causes, or as the result of an accident."

"We just went through that, Giles," Percival said patiently. "No disease kills in one second. Whatever was wrong with him, if there was anything wrong, he died of a broken neck. That's for sure. I seen lots like that; I know."

"Tell me something, Mr. Sullivan," Faber said. "If you was Mrs. Kruger's lawyer, would you take the case on contingency?" He looked into Giles' eyes. "See, that's what I mean. Now I know you're all shook up, but have you thought of this? Let's say, Mr. Sullivan, it was an accident. To your guest, in your home, and you got paid for his board. He wasn't there because he wanted to be there, but because you forced him—all right, *induced* him, okay?—into staying in your house, almost like a prisoner. You fed him the rich foods, which was bad for him, and you gave him the Scotch. You provided the cane that didn't work and it was on your stairs that he broke his neck, which prevented him from winning the contest. Tell me, Mr. Sullivan, how much insurance do you carry? Eighteen million? Plus heartache, pain, loss of husband's services? Future earnings? Kruger had a good business going, you said. So do you really want a verdict of accidental death, Mr. Sullivan?"

Giles was silent, thinking madly. Trying to think rationally. There was no escape. "I could still be sued by Mrs. Kruger even if the M.E. said 'death by unknown causes.'"

Faber leaned forward earnestly. "Mr. Sullivan, even if I could influence what the M.E. decided, I wouldn't. That would open a bigger can of worms than you could imagine."

"The lieutenant's right," Percival said. "Maybe you'd be better off if the M.E. said it was murder."

"How would that help, Percival?"

"Why, if we found the murderer, you couldn't be sued for having a loose carpet or for not enough light on the stairs or for giving Kruger too much high-cholesterol food."

"We?" Giles was completely unnerved. "The police will never solve a crime like this one. They're not set up to do it. They *can't* do it."

"Then you do it," Percival said. "You can do it, Giles; look what you did with the last one."

"And if I do, how do I keep Mrs. Kruger from sueing me for inviting a murderer into my house to kill her husband?"

"One problem at a time, Giles. First things first. Find the murderer and then we worry about the other little problems."

23

"**S**O YOU'RE CALLING OFF THE TWELVE O'CLOCK PUZZLE session?" Lila asked.

"What else can I do?" Giles was pacing around the study.

"We have to collect Puzzle Number Three *sometime* today," Isabel said, "as close to noon as possible. Regardless of the obstacles, it's important to keep to the pattern of the contest so as not to give any of the heirs an excuse to make trouble."

"Excuses they don't need," Lila said. "One of them already did."

"You're certain it was murder?" Isabel asked.

"What else? You got six creeps in a mansion, an Agatha Christie–type desert island setup, and right after the last lap of the race for eighteen million is done, one of them dies accidentally. *Accidentally?* My youngest grandson would die laughing, and he's only four."

"If you know that much," Giles said, "will you also tell me who did it?"

"Right now, no. But leave me alone in a locked room with each one, and I'll tell you."

"Violence? You, Lila?"

"Jewish grandmothers don't use violence, Giles; we're not built for it. Also, it sometimes doesn't work. We use a different kind of coercion. Our torture is the worst kind: guilt."

"Guilt won't work on a crew like this," Isabel said. "Not only aren't they children of Jewish mothers, they're all, from what they've said about each other, thoroughly nasty characters who wouldn't feel guilty even if you caught them red-handed slicing up their own parents, much less killing a second cousin-in-law."

"Isabel's right," Giles said. "Much as I trust your intuition, Lila, we need concrete evidence."

"Evidence you need? Okay, try this. Kruger's room was on the third floor. He was found on the third-floor stair landing. So where did he fall *from?*"

"The fourth floor, of course."

"So what was he doing on the fourth floor, Giles? Taking a breath of fresh air? Exercise? Looking for a midnight snack? Peeping through keyholes? What?"

"It's clear he was visiting someone on the fourth floor. Victoria van Broek, Gloria Raffa, or Sondra Stempel. Are you saying one of them must have killed him?"

"Why must have? If *he* could climb up one flight of stairs, Eileen Ashe or Richard Deddich couldn't? Anyone who noticed him going upstairs could easily wait in the corridor, either the one alongside the stair or the one transverse to it."

"Couldn't he then see whoever was waiting?" Isabel objected.

"How? Going upstairs, he had to concentrate on climbing the stairs. What with his weight and the cane and the bursitis, it had to take most of his concentration. So if it was Eileen or Richard who peeked through the cracked-open door and saw him, either one—they're both young—could have sneaked up the stairs fast and seen which room Kruger went into. Then it was just a matter of waiting in the right place. If he entered Victoria's room, or Sondra's, the third-floor killer waited in front of Gloria Raffa's room, next to the elevator, probably on the landing of the stair going up. If Kruger went into Gloria's room, at the front of the house, he waited, or she, in the back corridor, in front of Sondra Stempel's room. Either way, he was out of sight as Kruger left the other room."

"That doesn't sound too good to me," Isabel said. "The corridors may be unlit, but there's always a small spill of light from the stair, and Kruger would have carefully peeked out of whatever room he was leaving before venturing out into the stair going back down. And if he was hiding in front of someone's door, Sondra's or Gloria's, and for whatever reason one of them opened the door, he would be in a very embarrassing position and would never, forever after, be able to kill Kruger."

"You're right, Isabel," Lila agreed. "What's more, Kruger

wouldn't be the one to even peek through the door when he was ready to leave; it would have to be his accomplice. So the only place the killer could have waited was where I said before, on the landing of the stair going up to the fifth floor. Hidden by the elevator on one side and the partition along-side the stair on the other, he couldn't be seen from the door of any room. So the killer waited there until he heard the door open and, when Kruger was at the head of the stairs going down to his floor, the killer quietly ran there and pushed Kruger hard. Presto, the perfect crime."

"The same thing," Isabel said, "could have been done more easily if the killer was already on the fourth floor: Victoria, Sondra, or Gloria. All any one of them had to do was crack open her door and keep an eye on the area near the head of the stair."

"I didn't say it couldn't have been done by any one of the five," Lila said, "just showing how it was done."

"Hold on, there," Giles said, entering the discussion. "Victoria is very small. And old. Kruger was large. She couldn't push him very easily. Besides, she has arthritis in her hands."

"You don't have to push with your hands," Lila said. "You can push with your forearms, elbows, shoulders, your whole body. She was in the best position; her door is practically opposite the stair landing going down. Kruger may have been big, but he was also fat, unstable. He had a painful hip and a cane. Practically a pushover."

"If he was holding the handrail," Giles contended, "nei-ther Victoria nor Eileen could have pushed him down. None of them could, not even Richard."

"He wasn't holding the handrail," Isabel said. "It was his right hip that was bad, so he had to have the cane in his left hand to balance the bad leg, and the handrail would be on his left."

"He could have held on to the handrail with his left hand and carried the cane in his right hand."

"The cane was found on his left, Sullivan."

"It could have fallen there when he fell, Macintosh."

"Children, children," Lila chided. "Take it easy. At this stage, we have to keep all possibilities open. There's no way to eliminate any of the suspects yet. We have to talk to them first."

"We can't do that until Lieutenant Faber finished getting statements from each of them, which could take hours."

"Maybe if we let your brother interrogate them . . . ?"

"Percival? Never. He'd turn my home into a KGB prison."

"He'd get results," Lila pressed.

"I'm sure of that," Giles said, sarcastically. "But what would we do with five confessions?"

"Okay, Giles, we'll do it ourselves. How about if we have them come in here, one at a time, to hand in Puzzle Number Three, and quiz them?"

"No good, Lila," Isabel said. "The three of us sitting behind a desk and the suspect standing there before us answering questions? Like a Chinese People's Court? With this crowd? Forget it."

"Besides," Giles pointed out, "I don't think it's a good idea to let them think it's all right to start wandering around the house right now, talking to each other. Let's keep them isolated in their own rooms for a while longer, wondering who said what, who saw whom during what, who knows what. Then, when we interview them, they'll be much more likely to be truthful."

"Very good, Giles," Isabel said. "Are you sure you didn't take any courses with the KGB?"

"Okay," Lila said, "I'll go with that. As soon as the cops finish, we'll go around interrogating the creeps. That I'm going to enjoy."

"Sorry, Lila," Isabel said, "but not you. First of all, two is better than three; less imposing and makes for easier conversation. Even more important, you're the judge of the contest. With you deciding who gets the eighteen million, none of them will admit to even having pimples as an adolescent."

"You're not going to leave me here alone all day, not knowing what's going on, unless you want me to explode all over your fancy furniture. I want you to come back here after every interview and tell me everything."

"Make that every two interviews," Isabel said, "and it's a deal; we have a limited amount of time today before we collect Friday's puzzles. But you don't have to sit here and do nothing. Work on the hidden message."

"What do you think I was doing all last night, huh? Sleeping?"

"So sleep now, Lila; nothing's going to happen for the next couple of hours. Call Oliver and ask him to send up some hot chocolate."

"Hot chocolate? I'll tell him to send up a good-looking middle-aged cop. You stick to your hobbies, Isabel; I'll stick to mine."

24

"**K**RUGER DIED OF A BROKEN NECK," PERCIVAL ANnounced, putting down his coffee cup, "subject to the official autopsy report, which won't be available for a while yet." Oliver put another plate of chocolate-chip cookies on the kitchen table and refilled Lieutenant Faber's cup as well.

"Can't you rush him a little?" Giles asked.

"I rushed him a lot, Giles, but I'm retired now, have no official standing. The lieutenant could throw me out right this minute and he'd have every right to."

"I'd never do that, Chief," Lieutenant Faber said. "You were the top when I was starting out and, as far as I'm concerned, you'll always be the chief."

"Thanks, Faber, I really appreciate that. Keep on the way you're going and you got a good shot at the job yourself." Percival turned back to Giles. "The M.E. is really cooperating, Giles. If he doesn't find anything tricky, we could have the report early this afternoon. Unofficially."

"He didn't say whether it was an accident or not, did he? Or if he thought it was murder?"

"That's not for him to decide; he just reports the cause of death. The lieutenant here decides if a crime has been committed."

"I'm not making any official decision," Faber said, "until I get the M.E.'s report. And I want to check over the notes of my interviews."

"Did you learn anything," Isabel asked, piling her plate full of cookies, "from your interrogations of our five suspects?"

Faber smiled. "They're not suspects, Miss Macintosh, unless there's been a crime committed. And what I learned from them was exactly what I expected. No, poor Mr. Kruger didn't visit me last night; no, I saw nothing, heard nothing, suspected nothing, and it's a terrible shame that poor Mr.

103

Kruger fell down the stairs but they do say that most accidents happen in the home, don't they? And I can't imagine what he was doing up on the fourth floor; I was fast asleep shortly after ten o'clock. Foul play? Why would anyone want to kill dear Uncle Albert?"

"They're all lying, Lieutenant Faber. Giles told you the background."

"Oh, sure, they're lying, Miss Macintosh; they always do the first time around. The next time around, a few discrepancies will show up. I'll use those to find a few other discrepancies, and eventually, someone will break."

"There won't be a next time, Lieutenant," Isabel said decisively. "You know it and I know it. The medical examiner is going to find that Albert Kruger officially died of a broken neck and that this injury is perfectly consistent with his falling down the stairs. He'll find that Kruger did have atherosclerosis and may even have had a spasm of the coronary arteries, but as to what caused that, he has no way of knowing. So he has to make it 'accidental death,' he has no choice, and you have no suspects to question."

"You're probably right, Miss Macintosh," Faber said ruefully, "but what can I do about that?"

"One of them killed him." Isabel was vehement. "You know it and I know it. Are you going to let him get away with that?" Oliver quickly put more cookies on her plate.

"I'm a police officer, Miss Macintosh; I can only do what the regulations permit. It's the right thing, too. Imagine what it would be like if the police had unlimited authority, no restraints. I wouldn't want to live in a country like that, Miss Macintosh, and neither would you."

"What about you, Percival?" she asked. "You're not a policeman now. Are you going to let him get away with murder? The murderer? Right here in your brother's house?"

Percival looked down into his coffee cup. "My way—it only works with known criminals, professionals, guys I can put a little pressure on, make deals with. These are solid citizens, Isabel. I can't lock them away. I can't even question them. Any one of them can tell me to go f—fly a kite, and there's nothing I can do about it."

"Then I'll do it. Me and Giles. Giles and I. They can't leave the house until one of them finds the secret message; so far Lila, Giles and I don't even have an idea where to start. Unless there's a breakthrough, they'll be here until Wednesday noon. They can't refuse to talk to me; I'll threaten to tell Lila about their lack of cooperation and anything else I feel like making up. Anyone who doesn't jump when I say so, he better kiss his chances at eighteen million good-bye."

Percival looked at Faber. Faber nodded and said, "Okay. Sounds good to me. I'd like you to tell me everything you find out, though, no matter how unimportant it sounds to you. But you have to understand that I can't be coming here. You'll report to the chief here; he's family, got a good excuse to come here every day. In fact, my not being here could be a big plus. They'll talk to you a lot more openly than they'll talk to me."

Percival nodded. "Yeah, it'll feel good to be working again. Also"—he looked meaningfully at Giles—"maybe it'll give us a chance to ... you know what I mean."

Giles nodded in turn. "I'd like that, Percival. I'd like it very much."

"I have to get back to the house," Faber said. "I've shot half the morning here already. Anything else anyone'd like to tell me?"

"Oliver has his own spy system set up," Isabel said, "with the maids. He knows more about what goes on here than anyone else."

"Very little to report, Miss Isabel. Carmen told me that Miss Victoria's attitude toward servants has changed very little. Further, she washed her own pantyhose and watered the cacti. Cacti can be killed by overwatering, and I will inform Miss van Broek that she is to leave all domestic chores to the domestics. Miss Stempel ordered pie and ice cream at nine o'clock and milk and chocolate-chip cookies at nine-fifty-five. She left crumbs all over the carpet. Miss Raffa ordered two more legal-size yellow pads and one of quad-ruled paper. She burnt large quantities of paper in her wastebasket and flushed the ashes down the toilet bowl. The footman will have to help Agnes clean the soot off the bathroom walls. Mr. Deddich made no special requests and did not cause trouble in any way. Miss Ashe is still leaving everything where it falls, but there are no papers or scraps in her room. It is probable that she spends a good deal of time tearing them into small pieces and flushing them down the toilet bowl."

"Kruger," Percival said, "that's the one I'm interested in."

"Mr. Kruger's room had the solved puzzles on his desk, but no papers. Very few sheets had been torn off his pad and, presumably, he had disposed of them in the toilet bowl, too. He ordered a double single-malt Scotch at nine and another at ten. I served that one myself. He seemed highly agitated at that time."

"What did he say, Oliver?"

"Nothing, Mr. Percival, not even 'thank you.' He seemed to have a serious problem on his mind."

"Yeah, like should he take a chance on going up to the fourth floor, visiting somebody."

"Begging your pardon, Mr. Percival, but he did not necessarily go up to the fourth floor. I read a great deal, mostly whodunits, and I believe it is possible to break someone's neck and arrange the body so that it appears a fall downstairs was the cause."

"Can you see Gloria Raffa or even Sondra Stempel having the strength to do that, Oliver?"

"It is not only a matter of strength, Mr. Percival, but a matter of knowledge and leverage. In times of crisis, people often find the strength to do what they must. But I suggest we do not confine ourselves only to the people residing on the third floor. Just as Mr. Kruger could have gone upstairs, someone from the fourth floor could have gone downstairs."

"Eileen Ashe? Richard Deddich?" Giles looked doubtful. "Or Victoria van Broek? With her arthritis?"

"It is only in her hands, sir; she is quite spry otherwise. A neck can be broken by gripping it in the crook of an arm and twisting properly. Or so I understand from my novels."

"Yes, Oliver," Giles said, "I'll take your word for it. But one thing is certain; Albert Kruger left his room himself. Voluntarily. For his own reasons. If the murderer had met with Kruger in Kruger's own room, he could have killed him there, with far less risk."

"Possibly he did, sir, and then carried the body out and placed it on the stair. It would have been very difficult to kill Mr. Kruger in his own room, leave the body there, and make it look like an accident."

"Carry him out, Oliver? Kruger must have weighed two hundred fifty pounds."

"Yes, sir, but he also had a large stiff suitcase with caster wheels on the bottom. I'm sure any of our guests could have managed with that."

"Wait a minute, Oliver," Percival said. "Kruger was killed by having his neck broken. How do you do that in his own room?"

"I can answer that," Isabel said. "Don't forget, Kruger was in his pajamas."

"Also dressing gown and slippers," Percival added.

"Those could have been put on later, Percival; don't interrupt me." Isabel's voice took on a seductive, girlish quality. "'I know you're a very experienced lover, Albie, but here's one I'll bet you've never seen. Just lie across the bed and let your head dangle over the side. Turn it all the way to the left. Now I'll take off my bra and put my right arm underneath to hold your head steady. I'll lean over and hold your chin—oops, lost my balance. Good-bye, Mr. Kruger, nice to have known you.' Would that work, Oliver?"

"Indubitably, Miss Isabel. I was not aware you read whodunits, too."

Faber got up abruptly. "I'm leaving. The longer I stay here, the worse it gets. We now know for sure that Kruger either went up to the fourth floor or he stayed on the third floor. He went into someone's room or somebody came to his room or they met in the hall. He was either pushed downstairs from the fourth floor or killed on the third-floor landing or in his own room. And it could have been done by any of five people, including a crippled old lady, a little schoolgirl, or a skinny pencil pusher. You coming, Chief?"

Percival got to his feet heavily. "Yeah, I'd like to go through your notes. And don't forget, Lieutenant, it could also have been an accident."

"Yeah," Faber said, "but why to me?"

25

"**Y**OU HAVEN'T FOUND THE SECRET MESSAGE YET?" ISA-
bel teased. "Lila Quinn, Blitz-Scrabble champion of the
world?" She and Giles sat down at the study table, opposite
Lila.

"That's a handicap," Lila said, "with crap like this. My
mind works intuitively; if I don't see it right away, I'll never
see it. What this job needs is a slow, steady, plodding mind.
Like the guy who constructed the puzzles. That's what he
was like, wasn't he, Giles?"

"Cornelius van Broek? Yes, he wasn't a bit like you, Lila,
but he wasn't stupid either. He had a methodical mind. He
was not fast, not intuitive; he was logical. Very careful about
what he said and wrote, very exact, very precise, in both
business and his personal life. Very literal; he said what he
meant and meant what he said. It might take him a while,
but he always came up with the right answer. He made his
own decisions; never let anyone manage his money for him.
Of course, it was a much simpler world, then."

"Which of the five," Isabel asked, "is most like him?"

"Of the *six,* Albert Kruger. Not just physically, though
there is a strong family resemblance, but psychologically,
too. Kruger was a businessman who slowly built up his chain
of franchise outlets and, if he hadn't been killed, would have
been a very wealthy man ten years from now."

"I wish we had him now," Lila said, "to try these puzzles
on. I don't think any of us has the right type of mind for
this, not even you, Giles."

"I'm not so sure Kruger was the right type either," Isabel
said. "Why would he be out of his room late at night, except
to try to make a deal to cooperate with one of the other
contestants? If he had found the message, he'd be locked in
his room until this morning. I know we mentioned sex before,

108

but I don't believe any businessman would risk being thrown out of the contest just for a quick roll."

"You'd be surprised what people will risk," Lila said, "for motives that you and I would consider ridiculous. Still, if he had found the message, why should he be running around the house? And if one of the others had the message, why talk to Kruger at all?"

"Obviously, none of them had found the message yet," Giles said. "Otherwise one of them would have demanded to see Lila, with us as witnesses."

"Not necessarily," Lila said. "If I had decoded the message and found out that Kruger had been killed the night before, I'd keep my mouth shut for a day or two, even if it meant that I'd be risking somebody else beating me to the inheritance. I wouldn't want to call attention to myself at that particular time and I especially wouldn't want the cops to think that Kruger had decoded the message and that I had killed him to get it."

"You must be really tired, Lila," Isabel said. "If I had the secret message, I'd speak up right now; you can hire an awful lot of lawyers for eighteen million. Then, as far as anyone knew, it was an accident. Moreover, none of the five was told that anyone had been killed; just that they had to stay in their rooms."

"The killer knew," Lila replied, "and he knew it was no accident either. And our creeps are smart enough to know that the cops don't interview them just for practice."

"Do you think the murderer had decoded the message?" Giles asked. "If he had, why bother killing Kruger? And if Kruger had decoded the message, why give it to anyone else? Either possibility leads to another mystery."

"Clearly Kruger didn't find the message," Isabel said. "But maybe he had an idea, an approach, and needed someone else's specialized knowledge to decode the message."

"That narrows down the field a lot," Lila said. "Victoria knows how her father thinks, Gloria is the smartest and the quickest of them all, Sondra has an encyclopedia in her head, Richard is an accountant, and Eileen is a law student. What kind of specialized knowledge would Kruger need?"

"I don't know," Giles said. "Maybe none. Maybe this was part of his campaign to talk to each one of his relatives, to quietly set up the sort of collaborative arrangement he asked me about in Henry Winston's office. He would visit first one, then another, until he had them all signed up. Then, regardless of who found the solution, each heir would get three million dollars."

"How?" Isabel asked. "We figured out, the first day, Wednesday—could it have been only three days ago?—that one person, working with Victoria van Broek, could be her heir and share that way. But that's *one* person."

"So Victoria can't have *five* heirs?" Lila asked.

"It's a lot harder to put together six people than two," Isabel said. "A hundred times as hard. What do you do if you come to, say, Richard Deddich and say that the five of you have made a deal. He's not stupid. He immediately calls Lila and tells her that the other five have broken the rules, would she please disqualify them at once and, since he's the only heir left, would she please crown him as the heir that most closely resembles Cornelius van Broek and not fool around with hidden messages. No, I don't see Kruger, or any of the others, putting himself in that position."

"Yeah, I guess you're right, Isabel," Lila admitted. "I don't even see Kruger approaching Victoria for that. She's a sharp old lady, and she'd realize that she'd have only hours to live after she won the contest if she made a will in Kruger's favor."

"Maybe we have it backwards," Giles said. "Everyone's thinking in terms of Victoria being the most likely to die of natural causes, but she seems to be in pretty good condition to me. Why isn't Albert Kruger more likely? He's only a year younger than Gloria Raffa, and he's a smoker and very overweight. With his personality, he could get a heart attack any day. When he had indigestion at supper last night, I saw his face. *He* thought he had a heart attack. So maybe it was Kruger who was approached by one of the others."

"Then why kill him now?" Lila asked. "Before he inherits the eighteen million and before he writes a new will? No, Giles, we're missing something. None of these scenarios is really sound."

"Isn't it possible," Isabel asked, "that Kruger was approached about a cooperative effort and, seeing the opportunity to get rid of one contestant, said he would turn in the approacher? Whereupon the approacher killed him?"

"Not a chance," Lila said firmly. "First of all, Kruger

wanted the cooperation. But more than that, would he risk turning in a contestant just to improve his chances from sixteen to twenty percent? If he could do it for free, why not? But he'd now have to worry about one of the others claiming that Kruger had approached him with the same deal. Since it was Kruger's idea in the first place, he'd be the most vulnerable to such an accusation. At a minimum, it would cause him a great deal of headache. But the clincher is, was Kruger so stupid, even if he decided to turn in the other guy, to *tell* the guy at that time, that he intended to turn him in? Never. No, that one won't fly either."

"All right," Giles said decisively, "we're not getting anywhere, but at least we're eliminating some dead-end paths." He looked at his watch. "We have time to interview one or two of them before lunch. Lila, you stay here and study the puzzle some more. Don't do it methodically; don't try to do what isn't natural for you. Just relax and let inspiration strike you. I'll tell Oliver to continue keeping the five in their rooms and serve them lunch there, too."

"What about collecting yesterday's puzzles, Giles? It has to be done soon."

"We'll do that after the interviews. With luck, we'll be done by three or so. After we talk to them all, there's no point in keeping them isolated."

"I guess not," Lila said. "But one suggestion, Giles. Let the service be a little less perfect; have Oliver's assistant take a nap this afternoon."

"The footman? Whatever for?"

"Yeah, the footman. So he can stay on the steps between the third and the fourth floors tonight. Just in case."

26

"**W**HY AM I BEING KEPT HERE LIKE A PRISONER?" EILEEN Ashe demanded of Isabel and Giles.

"You volunteered," Giles said mildly. "You can leave any time you wish."

"I volunteered to stay in this house and abide by the rules of the contest, Mr. Sullivan; I did not volunteer to be locked in my room."

"The door was not locked from the outside, Miss Ashe. Your ability to adjust to minor inconveniences was being tested. Adaptability, you see. And your reaction will not win you any points. If you woke at seven, you've been in here a little over four hours, during which you were served an excellent breakfast, your room was vacuumed, your clothes cleaned, pressed and hung up, your bed made and your various needs and whims attended to. Hardly the tortures of the damned, I would say."

"How much longer will this go on?" Eileen was again the sweet young schoolgirl, Giles noted, his remark about points having sunk in.

"You will be served lunch at the regular time, Miss Ashe, and sometime later this afternoon, your filled-out puzzle, yesterday's puzzle, will be collected. After that, you will be free to leave your room. Or you can leave right now, if you wish; Carmen will help you pack."

"There is really no need for threats, Mr. Sullivan." Eileen was now completely in command of her role. She showed a sweet, tremulous, little-girl smile. "I was merely seeking an explanation for the sudden change in routine. It startled me. Then, when the detective started asking me all those questions about where I was and what I did..."

"It was for your own protection, Eileen." Giles fell in with the game. "Mr. Kruger died during the night." He watched her face carefully.

"Uncle Albert? Oh, my God!"

Isabel took over. "You got an 'A' in dramatic arts, Eileen? Pretty good for an amateur, but it lacked the professional touch. Kruger wasn't your uncle, was he?"

"Not really, but that's what we called him. And I resent your implicit accusation, Miss Macintosh. I was truly shocked by Uncle Albert's death."

"Maybe you were and maybe you weren't, but you weren't just now." Isabel leaned back in her chair, relaxed and confident. This was an old situation for her. "I was dean of students for five years, Eileen, and I've seen and heard everything. From better actresses than you'll ever be. When did you find out about Kruger's death?"

Eileen looked left and right, then down. "When the police came. There was so much noise that I just had to open the door a tiny bit. Carmen was at the end of my corridor; she couldn't see me at all. I heard everything, then I locked my door so the killer couldn't get at me."

"With all the police around? Aren't you the one who was going to stab anyone who tried to come into your room?"

"Uncle Albert wasn't stabbed, if that's what you're getting at. He was pushed down the stairs."

"Pushed? Why do you say 'pushed'?"

"If you think it was an accident, Mr. Sullivan, why are you interrogating me? He was pushed, all right, by someone on the fourth floor. This floor."

"Not necessarily, Eileen. We've figured out that it was probably done by someone on the third floor. Who do you think it was?"

"Aunt Gloria or Aunt Sondra? If you're sure it was one of them, it had to be Aunt Gloria."

"Why her, Eileen?"

"She runs a business, makes decisions, exploits people."

"I think," Isabel said, "that it could only have been done by someone on the fourth floor."

"Great Aunt Victoria or Richard? I don't believe it."

"Or you, Eileen. Richard doesn't have the nerve, and Victoria is too weak."

"I didn't. I couldn't. I'm not strong enough to do anything like that; I'm a girl."

Isabel looked at her, disgusted. "I hate women who want equal rights and then fall back on that 'But I'm just a weak little girl' crap. Do you want me to leave Victoria van Broek off the list of suspects, too? She's even smaller and weaker than you are."

Eileen looked flustered. "Of course. If you leave me off the list, you have to leave her off, too."

"She's not off the list," Isabel said, "and you aren't either. And we know it could have been done by a weak woman, there are several ways, so our only problem is how to get Kruger into your room."

"I wouldn't let anyone into my room; he could steal my notes. Besides, Mr. Sullivan said that any collusion and we'd both be disqualified."

"Only if you were caught, Eileen. What I was thinking of—you knew Kruger was a lecher." Isabel did not put that as a question.

Eileen considered this for a few seconds and came up with the nonincriminating answer. "All men are lechers."

"You forgot to add, Eileen 'if you're young and beautiful like me.' Come off it, Eileen. Either talk straight or I end the conversation right now and do two things. One, tell Lila Quinn what a big faker you are and two, tell the police how you could have gotten Kruger to come to your room."

Eileen looked daggers at Isabel, but said nothing.

"There are interior phones, Eileen. You ring Kruger and say, in a baby-doll voice, 'Oh, Uncle Albert. I'm so frightened. Just as I got undressed I heard a noise and I'm so afraid to be all alone dressed in nothing but my nightgown and no man to protect me, so would you please . . . I'll leave the door unlocked; make sure nobody sees you.' How's that for a scenario, baby doll?"

Eileen looked at her contemptuously. "You didn't do that very skillfully at all, Miss Macintosh," she said in a flat voice. "You need more experience with men, or lessons, or both. You have to be less explicit. If you promise too much, they can get very angry if you don't deliver. If you let them write the fantasy, you're much better off. Sure I could have done it that way; I probably could have gotten even a cold fish like Richard to come to me, too. But I didn't. What for?"

"To get their leads, to find out the dead ends, to pool knowledge, to steal solutions. Or to kill them, one at a time, to increase your odds of winning."

Eileen put on her big horn-rimmed glasses. Suddenly she

ooked like a scholar. "You're not thinking, Miss Macintosh. None of them knows a thing. If any one of them had found he message, you'd have heard about it loud and clear. First ne wins, so if you've found the message, you want it recorded y Mrs. Quinn right this second. Why take chances, I mean, hat one of the others would find it five minutes later? As or reducing the odds, do you think I would be so stupid as o kill someone, to risk a murder charge, just so I could have one-in-five chance rather than a one-in-six? And help the ther four left as much as I was helped? Give them a free ide? As it stands now, if I lose, I'm no worse off than I was efore. The other way, I could end up in jail. For eighteen nillion, yes, maybe I'd take the risk. But to reduce the odds little? You'd have to be real stupid to figure that way. I am ot stupid."

I didn't think you were, Giles said to himself as he and sabel left, but I didn't realize how smart you were either.

27

"YOU REALLY STRAIGHTENED HER OUT, ISABEL," GILES said in the hall. "I never saw you like that before."

"If you lived with me at Windham," Isabel replied, "you'd have lots of chances to see me like that. Or better. Or worse, depending on how you look at it. I hardly deal with students now; most of my trouble is with the bigger game. Not better and not necessarily smarter game, but always more experienced, more tricky, and even less scrupulous than the students. With more at stake. Sometimes I feel like a lion tamer. With a *very* small whip. And a bull's-eye painted on my back."

"I don't think I want to see you like that, Isabel; it gives me the feeling that you don't really need me. Let's not talk in the hall; come downstairs to our room."

"No, let's get this over with; I just want to take a few minutes' break. We'll stand on the stair landing and talk quietly. Of course I need you, Giles, for so many things. You can't imagine.... What I don't need you for, what I don't *want* you for, is protection, shielding, what your Middle Ages–chivalry-type mind sees as your masculine duty. I'm just as tough as you are, Giles; tougher, in some ways. And the trouble is, even though I love your wanting to take care of me, I resent it when you try to. Can you understand that?" She put her arms around him and looked up into his eyes.

"If we were married, or even when we're together, I want to...if you have a problem, I want to help. If I have a problem, Isabel, I'd appreciate your help. If we have a problem, we *both* do what *we* can. If we were married, there'd be no *my* problem, *your* problem; it would be *our* problem and we'd both do what we could."

"Isn't it that way now, Giles?" She put her head on his chest; he held her closely.

"Yes, when we're together. But we're apart so much, you hardly know what I do, and I share almost nothing of the acting president of Windham University."

"You'd die up there, Giles, as Mr. Acting President Macintosh."

"What I had in mind, Isabel, was that you come—"

"Exactly. Look, we've discussed this before and it always ends in a fight. Let's leave this for another time, Giles. Talk to me about something less important. What's your opinion about Eileen Ashe as murderer?"

"She's a prime suspect, Isabel; that innocent look had me fooled. I didn't realize how smart and how strong she is."

"Most men don't realize that about most women most of the time. Speaking as a man, do you think she could have gotten Deddich to come to her room, as she claimed?"

"Speaking as a man, she could have gotten any man to come to her room in thirty seconds. Except me, of course."

"You're just saying that because you value your life, Giles. Give me a moment to freshen up my lipstick and run a comb through my hair."

"You look all right to me, Isabel."

"A Cary Grant you'll never be, Sullivan, but your heart's in the right place. It's not for you, dear; I want to distract Richard Deddich while you give him the third degree. If she can do it, I can do it. I hope."

28

"OF COURSE I KNEW SOMETHING WAS WRONG," RICHARD Deddich said, "when Carmen told me to stay in my room, but I didn't know it was Uncle Albert." Isabel was more annoyed than she thought she'd be when, after a quick glance at her, Richard had kept his eyes on Giles. This is crazy, she thought, I'm old enough to be his mother. What the hell do I care what this insipid little bookkeeper thinks of me? And why do I always go through this, trying to prove myself, whenever I'm with Giles and we're talking with a beautiful young girl and he notices her? God, imagine how crazy I'd be if we were married. And living in Windham, with hundreds of them, thousands, all over the place. It's all Sullivan's fault, for not greeting me properly at the airport, sweeping me into his arms, mad with lust and . . .

"No, sir, I never left my room," Richard said. "I locked the door and worked on finding the secret message."

"Did you hear anything?"

"Not a sound, Mr. Sullivan, but the doors are thick, the carpets are heavy, and, as I said, I was concentrating."

"Did you receive any phone calls last night?"

"No, sir, nor make any either; not even for room service. I lead a very quiet life, usually, and particularly now, with so much at stake, I want to concentrate all my energies on the problem at hand."

"Do you find Eileen Ashe attractive?" Isabel was herself surprised that the question popped out. Ten more years, she thought, and I'll be a real crazy old lady. It's all Sullivan's fault for putting me into this stupid situation. All I wanted, all I needed, was a short vacation, a week of relaxation, sex, and chocolate. And love; to love and be loved.

Deddich raised his eyebrows slightly at the question, but a second later he resumed his bland face and voice. "I sup-

118

pose so, Miss Macintosh, by today's standards, but I really can't think of those things now. I must devote all my thoughts to finding the message."

"Today's standards, Richard? You talk as though your tastes are different. Would you say that Gloria Raffa is attractive?"

"I suppose so, Miss Macintosh, but we're related, and she's old enough to be my mother." Serves you right for asking, Macintosh; Gloria is six years younger than you are. "Why are you asking me these questions?"

Don't answer that, Macintosh, and for God's sake, don't ask him if he thinks *you're* attractive. "If either Gloria or Eileen called you, would you go to her room?"

"That depends on what it was for. Sickness, or something like that, certainly. I'd also call Oliver before I went, unless it was an emergency. I wouldn't want to be disqualified for collaboration. But I didn't go anywhere; I told you that. Did anyone say she saw me?"

"We haven't spoken to everyone yet," Isabel said, "but we'll find out soon enough."

"No one could have seen me. If anyone said she had, the police would have arrested me by now."

"The police are waiting for the medical examiner's report, Richard," Giles said. "Until they get that, they won't arrest anyone. But if you have anything at all to say, you're better off telling me first."

"Pardon my saying so, Mr. Sullivan, but that's absolute nonsense. People think that, because I'm not built like a football player, I can be conned and pushed around. I can't. I really can't. Do you think if I killed Uncle Albert, I'd be better off confessing to you? Why? Why should I confess to anyone, if I'm a murderer. How does confessing benefit me? And to you, of all people? The first thing you'd do, the first thing you'd *have* to do, would be to disqualify me for the inheritance. There's no way I'm going to confess, and you might as well accept that. If I'm guilty of a crime, I wouldn't, and if I'm innocent—and I am—why should I? So please, Mr. Sullivan, change the subject."

"As you wish, Deddich," Giles said. "Who do you think killed Albert Kruger?"

"You must realize that I have no direct knowledge and, as you've seen we're not exactly a very close family. But based on the past few days' observations, it is probably Aunt Sondra."

"Why her?"

"Personality. Sondra is a glutton; she has no willpower. Once she decides she wants something, she'll go through fire to get it. And she doesn't know when to stop. She *can't* stop. You want to try an experiment? Put a gallon of chocolate ice cream, not the good stuff that we had for dessert, but the cheapest junkiest trash you can find—put it in front of her. Right after a full meal." I finished a container of ice cream all by myself, Isabel remembered, right after a full meal. But it was Ping's special chocolate. And I don't think it was a full gallon. Much less. Much, much less. And I'm like that only about chocolate. And sex. I'm selective. "Sondra will finish that gallon of ice cream, before it melts. There are people who die every year—it's in the company's records—of ruptured stomachs from overeating. Sondra is like that. So if she decided that she must have that eighteen-million dollars and, if somehow, Albert stood in her way, she'd kill him, with no more thought than for the paper that had to be removed for her to get at that gallon of ice cream."

"How could killing Albert Kruger help her win the contest?"

"Directly? I have no idea. But indirectly? There's a big difference between a sixteen-and-two-thirds-percent chance and a twenty-percent chance. If you understood probability, you'd see that."

"Isn't there an even bigger difference between a twenty percent chance and a twenty-five percent chance?"

"Much. That's why I stay in my room at night with the door locked." Or maybe, Isabel thought, that's why you pointed the finger at Sondra Stempel. One more out of the way, and you have one chance out of four.

"If Miss Stempel is the murderer, Richard, why did she kill Kruger instead of someone else?"

"He was probably the only one out of his room last night. He's a real lecher, you know; I can tell." Richard turned to Isabel. "Now I understand why you asked me those questions, Miss Macintosh, about if I could be enticed out of my room by Eileen or Aunt Gloria. Miss Macintosh, let me assure you, the Queen of Sheba and Helen of Troy combined couldn't get me out of my room after ten o'clock at night or before seven in the morning, while the contest is on."

Blessings on thee, little man, for giving Giles a reasonable reason for my questions, for my craziness. "Do you have any evidence, Richard, to back up your accusation?"

"It wasn't an accusation, Miss Macintosh, just an opinion based on personality. But if there's a second body found tomorrow morning, just remember, a glutton doesn't know when to stop."

29

"**E**ILEEN AND RICHARD ARE STILL PRIME SUSPECTS?" LILA asked, as she served the open-faced sandwiches to Isabel and Giles. "So what else is new? Didn't I tell you they were all creeps?"

"Creeps are not necessarily murderers, Lila," Giles said.

"Necessarily, no; potentially, yes. Creeps do not get taken off the prime-suspects list until *after* the murderer is caught. Sorry, after the perpetrator is apprehended. Did you get anything useful?"

"Yeah," Isabel said dryly. "Albert Kruger was a lecher. Eileen Ashe knows how to use sex to gain her ends. Richard Deddich says he is too dedicatedly busy to kill anybody just now, but he thinks Sondra Stempel is the most likely to succeed."

"In other words, nothing."

"Did you get anywhere with the puzzle, Lila?" Giles asked.

"I got sick of looking at the damn thing and put the whole mess away. This is not my bag, Giles; I hope you realize that. I'm like a camera flash; if I don't get the picture immediately, I don't get it ever. You can't depend on me for slow, steady illumination."

"It would be very helpful, then, Lila," Isabel said, "if you would point your flashing pulsar mind at the murderer."

"I did. Did you think I could sit here, or anywhere, for an hour, doing nothing?"

"Nothing there, either?"

"Of course there is; when I can think of the right question, I always get the right answer. If there is an answer, that is. Not like this *farkockte* hidden message crap."

"*Farkockte?*"

"Forget it, Isabel; you'll never be able to use it at a faculty tea. You want Yiddish lessons or the murder?"

"The murder, please."

"All right, already, stop drooling. Look, you just pushed Albert Kruger down the steps. You haven't had much practice—who has?—pushing people down stairs, but it looks like his neck is broken. On the other hand, the light that's always on over the stairs is a small bulb—cheap is cheap, Giles—and you can't be sure he's dead. Could it be that Uncle Albert is, maybe, still alive? And if he is, is he going to get up two minutes later and tell that rotten Lila Quinn that you, the murderer, have committed conduct unbecoming a contestant?"

"If he does that," Isabel pointed out, "he has to admit he was in my room working on the puzzle and he gets thrown out, too."

"Not necessarily. He could say he was enticed to your room by the promise of untold delights and when he left, after sampling your fantastic repertoire, you suddenly decided to kill him to preserve your pristine reputation or because he didn't look like Paul Newman or because he forgot to eat his Wheaties or whatever. It doesn't matter. The point is, you have to make sure he's dead. How? By looking down, in the dim light, from the top of the stairs?"

"Okay, teacher, I get the point. I have to run downstairs to check. But didn't we also figure that it could have been done by someone from the third floor, too? Someone who's already down there? Or that Albert had his neck broken *before* he was flung down the stairs?"

"Sure, Isabel, any of these. The point is, he wasn't just pushed and forgotten about. The murderer had to have walked downstairs, or whatever, and checked Kruger's pulse or held a mirror in front of his mouth, something, to make sure he was dead. The murderer had to have contact with the corpse *after* the corpse became a corpse."

"That's obvious."

"Sure, *now* it's obvious. Okay, now what did Kruger have in his pockets, Giles?"

"Nothing, Lila. He was wearing a dressing gown. Just a handkerchief and a pencil."

"No paper? Not one piece? He assumed his murderer would have plenty of paper?"

"If it was one of the other five—"

"Of course it was, Giles, stop *phumpha*ing. No translation needed."

"Naturally, whoever he was going to visit would have plenty of paper."

"Naturally. So that means he was not going for lechery, right? Unless he took the pencil along to take notes on position fifty-three?"

"No, Lila, we're all agreed he went to somebody's room, upstairs or downstairs, to work on the hidden message."

"No, Giles, we've *established* that he went to whoever's room to work on the secret message. Okay? So having memorized, 'the eighteen million is buried three paces south of Ichabod Crane's tombstone in the Old Dutch Cemetery on Trinity Place,' he proceeds upstairs to share the goodies with Sondra Stempel because he's always had a crush on her and wants to impress her with his brilliance?"

"Don't get sarcastic, Lila; Giles and I are in very low spirits and we're highly pooped, to boot."

"Okay, Isabel, sorry. Anyway, if Kruger had found the message, why didn't he wake me up and demand that I sign, seal and notarize that he was the first to cross the finish line?"

"Maybe it wasn't that kind of message, Lila. Maybe it was like what you said before, directions how to dig up the treasure chest. Or something like that. Something physical."

"For eighteen million bucks, I would have hired six guys with shovels and six guys with guns and dug up my money *now,* right now, eleven P.M. on Friday night. Why take chances on a water-main break, or some other normal New York catastrophe? No, I think it is established that Kruger did *not* find the secret message. Now, did the murderer find it? Same reasoning. If he did, or she did, why invite Kruger to her boudoir? A Clark Gable he wasn't. So the murderer did not find the message either. Agreed?"

"Agreed, Lila. This flash of yours is not quite like lightning."

"The flash was fast. Telling it to you while you're wondering what kind of chocolate dessert Ping has provided special for your lunch, that's slow." Lila took another forkful of her sandwich. "So obviously Kruger picked up the phone to make an appointment to see the murderer, or the murderer called Kruger. Which?"

"Kruger called the murderer, Lila. It had to be. While Kruger was very bright, he didn't impress me as being an intellectual. I can't imagine any esoteric information or special skills that Kruger had, that anyone would need to find the message. But I can easily imagine Kruger needing one of them. Victoria knew her father's way of thinking; Gloria is very sharp-witted; Sondra has a head full of esoteric information; Eileen is a law student; Richard is a numbers expert."

"Numbers, Isabel? I hadn't considered Richard."

"We Cruciverbalists tend to think in terms of letters and words, but there's no reason why the message can't involve numbers. Or worse, the method of hiding the message may involve numbers."

"Okay, leave Richard on the list. I thought I had eliminated him, but okay, he stays. So we now have that Kruger calls the murderer and says that he has a terrific lead, he's broken the code, but he needs the murderer's special skills and/or knowledge. For this, they'll go halfies. The technique we'll work out later; I'm sure if Giles puts his mind to it, he can come up with some way to find a hole in the foolproof technique he planned. Kruger had to have done it. Once you know something can be done, Giles will work it out."

"Right," Isabel said. "Now I'll complete the scenario fast. The two of them work out the message—wait, I know an easy way that both of them can split the inheritance legally. Saturday morning they both come to your door, they swear they both got there absolutely simultaneously, they knock at the same time, and they both show you the correct solution simultaneously. Wouldn't you have to give them each half, Giles?"

Giles thought for a moment, then said, Reluctantly, "I'm afraid so. Of course, I'd like to discuss this with Henry Winston, with H. Randolph Williams, too, but I think you've hit on a workable technique, Isabel, for circumventing my procedure," he added, a little bitterly.

"Oh, don't sulk, Sullivan; every system can be broken, if you just get a hot flash. Right, Lila?"

Lila nodded. "Of course, we get back to the risk of trust between the collaborators."

"Sure, but we can work that out, too, if we want to bother. Anyway, back to the murder. Kruger and the killer work out the message and make neat copies, one for each. Kruger kisses the killer good-bye, limps out—I prefer Gloria to Sondra, especially for kissing good night—and Gloria suddenly realizes that, with Kruger dead, she gets an extra nine million, which is always useful. But why take the risk; isn't nine million enough? Sure it is, but on the other hand, with *Gloria* dead, Kruger gets an extra nine million and he always did have shifty eyes. Gloria suddenly gets a hot flash and realizes she's got a very short time to live. At seven A.M. Saturday, when she is joyously bounding down the stairs to Lila's room, Kruger is going to be lying in wait. And just as she reaches the third-floor landing going down to the second floor, Kruger pops out of his room, where he's been waiting with his eye glued to the just-cracked-open door—his room is right next to the landing as you come down—and pushes Gloria—no, pokes Gloria in the back with his cane and presto, no more trying to convince Lila they both got there at *exactly* the same time. In fact, he doesn't push—why have cane marks showing?—he uses the other end of the cane to *hook* Gloria's ankle and down she goes. While Gloria is lying there on the second-floor landing with a broken neck, Kruger limps down like a gentleman, plucks the paper with the secret message from Gloria's lifeless fingers, and hobbles to Lila's room. Then he presents the message, gets Lila to time stamp it, claims the eighteen million, and complains bitterly about the debris on the stairs he almost trips over and suggests that Lila reprimand Oliver for leaving dead bodies around where decent law-abiding citizens can trip over them. As soon as Gloria realizes this—it takes her all of a quarter of a second—she bounds out of her room just in time to give Albert the prophylactic push first. Correct, Lila?"

"You left out some parts, which I was getting to. When I get a flash, it's the whole picture. It wouldn't do for Kruger to be found with the secret message in his pocket, so Gloria, or whoever, slips quietly down the stairs and snatches the paper from Kruger's lifeless pocket. Otherwise, when she hands in her solution, someone might think she was not the first, and might even have done Kruger in. Now we come to the part that I was coming to before. If Kruger is alive, or even if she's not *sure* whether he is or not—and she damn well better make sure—she has to kill Kruger again."

"Carry him upstairs and push him down again?"

"Don't be funny, Isabel; I'm serious. You remember what we said about how, with Kruger in bed and his head hanging over the side, you put your arm around his head, grab his chin, and snap? Well, what better place to do it than when he's lying on the stairs unconscious?"

"Suppose he isn't unconscious?"

"Stunned he's got to be. The trick is to get downstairs fast, which you'd want to do anyway—cuts down your exposure time—and snap his neck, snatch the paper, and zip up again. Total time, maybe five or ten seconds."

Isabel gazed at Lila in admiration. "I do believe you've got it, Grandma. Now all we have to do is three more interviews and figure out whodunit. Which we will do. Right after dessert. Actually, why should we bother with the interviews? Whoever hands in the solved message, she's the killer."

"Not so fast, Isabel," Lila said. "Giles practically hasn't said a word all during lunch. And he still looks worried. Giles? Giles? What's the matter, *bubeleh?*"

"I'm thinking," Giles said gravely. "Everything you said sounds right. Is right, I'm sure. But there are a few problems. Handing in a correct message is not proof of guilt. We're not sure that Kruger and the killer solved the problem; maybe they just got started and found it was a dead end. Further, if they did solve the problem, or even got a good approach going, and Kruger intended to do away with his partner, why didn't he kill her in her own room? What was the point in waiting for the next day? He had privacy, time, and no witnesses. The body wouldn't have been discovered until eight o'clock the next day, or later. And if he didn't take this opportunity when he had it, why should quick-witted Gloria think he would try to kill her later, with maids, butlers, and other guests running up and down the stairs, watching. And if she was slow-witted and didn't think of that till much later, she could have called Lila to come to her room at six forty-five A.M., because that's when she just happened to find the solution and she was afraid to leave her room, thus leaving Kruger out in the cold for lateness, with nothing to say, since there were no witnesses to their midnight collaboration. And last, why did it have to be Kruger's partner who killed him? Couldn't it have been someone else, anyone, who, aroused by the victory dancing and singing in Gloria's room, or the headboard banging against the wall, or, in just going out for a midnight snack, peeked through the cracked-open door and, seeing a good opportunity to improve his odds in safety, pushed Kruger down the stairs?"

Isabel and Lila stopped smiling. Isabel eyed Giles coldly. "And that's another thing I don't like about you, Sullivan. You've just put us back to five prime suspects again. Thanks heaps."

30

"Now, really, Mr. Sullivan," Victoria van Broek said archly, "I can tell." They were seated around her bedroom table, sipping the tea she had ordered from Carmen. Victoria held her teacup in both hands, her knobbed fingers unable to hold the tiny handle. "I know an interrogation when I see one, even if it's done by a gentleman and a lady." This with a nod to Isabel. "I was interrogated after my husband passed away, and you're doing it now. Why? Is there a problem with Albert's death?"

"No, not really,"—Giles tried to put a good face on it. "We don't have the medical examiner's report yet, but everyone agrees that he died as a result of the fall."

"Ah, then you think he was pushed." Victoria thought for a moment. "I suppose that's possible, yes, given the lack of character of this younger generation. They're all in such a hurry; everything must be done *now*, achieved now."

"So you think Eileen or Richard are the most probable pushers?"

Victoria smiled sadly. "To me, Mr. Sullivan, Gloria and Albert are the younger generation. Eileen and Richard don't exist in my world. They move too fast; they—they blur."

"Sondra Stempel is only a few years older than Richard. Which generation is she?"

"The younger generation, Mr. Sullivan, the generation of my sisters' children, or the children I could have had. Richard and Eileen? When one doesn't have children, the grandchildren of your peers are only passing snapshots that all look alike."

"You think Gloria or Susan did it?"

"Did what, Mr. Sullivan? Pushed Albert down the stairs? Made Albert go upstairs? What makes you think he was pushed? Who could possibly gain by that? What did Albert have that was worth the effort? Or the risk?"

"The hidden message that is worth eighteen million dollars, Miss van Broek."

"Albert?" Victoria smiled sadly. "I'm sorry to disillusion you, Mr. Sullivan, but Albert was the least likely person to find the message. He may have *looked* like my father, but Albert was not very intelligent, not at all. Nor was he well educated."

"He seemed very confident of his skill as a crossword puzzler, Miss van Broek."

"Oh, that." She made it sound like an unimportant trifle. "Lots of practice, tenacity, and a good memory, is ninety percent of that skill. Your Mrs. Quinn, you said, is an expert solver of crosswords, yet it is painfully clear that she is not well educated, and she is certainly not a lady."

Giles was miffed. "Mrs. Quinn, who is a dear friend of mine, is very well educated and she is a lady in every sense of the word. Her actions can be ascribed to the exceedingly poor manners exhibited by the van Broek heirs."

"It may be true," Victoria admitted, "that some of us may have been a little too outgoing, but a lady is always a lady under any circumstances." She set her mouth firmly.

"Who do you think will find the hidden message?" Isabel asked.

"I will, of course," Victoria said confidently. "It's not the crosswords, you know; they're easy. I'm sure you'll find that we all—when you check the puzzles we filed—we all got them perfectly correct, even Albert. But I'm the only one who knows my father well. Even Gloria was only a child when he died. I don't waste my time trying every possible mathematical combination the way I'm sure Richard does. I think back to the old days, put myself back in the old days, and talk to my father. I make up conversations and I gradually lead them around to the secret message. Little by little, I'm getting closer and closer, and soon he will tell me where he hid it, and how he hid it."

"You realize, Miss Victoria," Giles said gently, "that you are talking to yourself?"

"Don't patronize me, Mr. Sullivan," she snapped, "of course I realize it. I'm not a crazy old lady yet. But when I speak in my father's voice, in my head, I do it with all his characteristics. I bring back all the memories, and when I've reconstructed him completely, perfectly, then he'll tell me the secret. Or, if you will, *I'll* tell the secret, but it will be correct."

"You have only until noon Wednesday, Miss van Broek," Giles reminded, "and it's already Saturday afternoon. I am required to give more tests so that, if no one gets your father's message, Mrs. Quinn can determine who most resembles your father's characteristics."

"Do you think, Mr. Sullivan, I would let my inheritance be disposed of by that—that foul-mouthed, vulgar person?" Her voice grew shrill. "No, Mr. Sullivan, I will bring you the message, my father's message, soon. Very soon. I can feel it."

"Did you open your door last night?" Isabel asked. "Even just to look out? Did you hear or see anything?"

"Certainly not. I was drowsing, visualizing my father. I wouldn't think of unlocking my door at night. Why ask me?"

"Well, your room is right at the head of the stairs. If you heard a noise and even looked through the keyhole, you might have seen who pushed Mr. Kruger down the stairs. If he was pushed."

"If he *were* pushed indeed, Miss Macintosh. To set your mind at rest, I did *not* hear anything, and I *never* look through keyholes. The location of my room was selected by Oliver, Mr. Sullivan's butler. And did it ever occur to you that, if Albert was pushed—he was a big man, quite big—it would have taken a mighty big push? Why didn't Albert yell or scream, then? If he had, then everyone in the house would have heard it, wouldn't they?"

"No one heard anything, Miss van Broek," Giles said. "If you would just calm down..."

"Then I suggest you stop bothering me. The reason he didn't scream, Mr. Sullivan, was that he slipped, pure and simple. One may scream in shock when one is pushed; one does not scream when one slips, because one is far too busy grasping for support. I suggest that you think of that after you leave. Good day to you, sir, and to you, too, Miss Macintosh."

31

"**S**HE'S RIGHT, GILES," ISABEL SAID, AS SOON AS VICTOria's door closed. "Why didn't Albert scream?"

"Let's go downstairs," Giles said, leading her straight ahead to the stair. "I don't want to talk where they can hear us. Victoria may never look through keyholes, but I'll bet she listens." They walked in silence down to the first floor. "The doors are thick, but they're not really soundproof."

They sat opposite each other at the dining-room table. Isabel put her elbows on the table and leaned forward. "It would take a really good push," she said, "to push a two-hundred-fifty pound man down the stairs. At the very least, a loud grunt from Albert?"

"If he were off balance," Giles countered, "just about to take the first step down, it would take less of a push."

"I don't see our killer having time to wait for the perfect moment to push Kruger. As I visualize it, she rushed out from wherever she was hiding and pushed as well as she could when she got to him. She didn't have time to measure the strength of the push either; she had to make sure she pushed hard enough for him to go over."

"He was using a cane and he did have a hip problem."

"We said before that he could have shifted the cane to his right hand and held on the handrail with his left hand."

"The cane was found on his left, Isabel."

"The cane was shifted by the killer when she came downstairs to make sure Kruger was dead and to steal the paper with the agreement on it, Sullivan. Why are you arguing with me? Do you really think I'm wrong?"

"I don't know; I'm just playing devil's advocate. You seem very sure it was a woman."

"I smell it. But even so, our suspects are four women and one man, so the odds favor a woman. Okay, Giles, why do you think Kruger didn't scream?"

"Drugged, maybe? In his tea? In Victoria van Broek's room while they were collaborating on the secret message?"

"If he was drugged, that would be pretty stupid. Who knows how long it would take to find the secret message? What good would it be if he passed out before they found the message? And wouldn't the medical examiner's report show any drugs? When will we get the report?"

"Pretty soon. In an hour or two, I would guess."

"Wouldn't Oliver have told us if any of them had sleeping pills, or anything like that?"

"Certainly. He probably would have confiscated them, if he found any, and doled them out one at a time, if there were dire need. But Kruger said he had drugs with him; presumably painkillers, anti-inflammatories, muscle relaxants. Couldn't several of those act as knockout drugs?"

"I doubt that, but even if they could, how would the killer get them from Kruger? And even if she could, seventeen of them might make the tea taste funny."

"Do you really think it was an accident, Isabel?"

"Of course not, but it kills me not to know why he didn't make any noise. Did you see any marks on the walls at the top landing? For a rope to be tied across at ankle level, I mean?"

"There are solid partitions on both sides of the stair; nothing to tie to. Nails or screw holes would be visible."

"I can't think of any situation, Giles, where he wouldn't make *some* noise if he was pushed downstairs. It's beginning to look as though one of our other techniques was used. He must have been killed in the killer's room."

"Noiselessly, Isabel?"

"Scenario 'A,' the one where he's lying on the bed with his head hung over the side as the scantily clad siren breaks his neck is beginning to look better and better to me."

"Gloria or Eileen?"

"Gloria. Don't ask me why. Intuition."

"I'll tell Oliver to check if she has a stiff suitcase with casters. What's Scenario 'B'?"

"Hit Kruger on the head, then drag him out and throw him down the stairs."

"I looked at the body rather carefully before the police came, and so did Oliver. There were no signs of broken skin.

He did shave his head, so it would have been visible."

"Couldn't he have been hit with something soft? A sand-bag, or a sap with lead shot, like the one Oliver has?"

"It would take several minutes for any of them—even Richard is no mass of muscle—to drag Kruger out, throw him downstairs, and go down and break his neck. A lump would have arisen by then. If any of them had a sap, or any possible weapon of any kind, Oliver would have reported it. He's very good at finding things like that."

"Same for an injection?"

"Definitely. No one brought any hypodermics into the house. Besides, that's something the medical examiner would pick up. Any of these techniques would immediately show murder, which seems to be the one thing the killer was desperately trying to avoid."

"Laughing gas? Ether? Something inhaled that would react with one of the drugs Kruger was taking that would make him sleepy? Antihistamines make me sleepy."

"Again, the medical examiner would probably find out. But more important, I don't think the killer knew he was going to kill Kruger before he came here. Or to kill anyone else. In fact, I doubt the killer knew he was going to kill Kruger until just before the murder. The earliest could have been when Kruger called up and made the appointment to get together. How could the killer know, the day before, that Kruger would leave his room at night? When did the killer prepare the anesthetic? How could he know what drugs Kruger was taking?"

"I know." For the first time, Isabel smiled. "Remember what I said before? About hooking Gloria's leg with Kruger's cane? Why couldn't Gloria hook Kruger's leg? Not with the cane; she ties a thin, strong cord to Kruger's ankle just before he leaves and, as soon as he starts down the stairs, she yanks."

"Aside from the rope burns, Isabel, it's awful. What does Gloria tell Kruger she's doing as she ties the cord on. Giving him a good luck charm? Preventing him from sleepwalking? If we're reaching for wild solutions like that, we're both in real bad shape. Let's have a hot chocolate before we go upstairs to Raffa and Stempel. We both need help."

32

"THE COPS WEREN'T ENOUGH?" GLORIA RAFFA OPENED the desk drawer and put all her papers out of sight before she waved Giles and Isabel to sit down. "You have to hound me, too?"

"This is your room," Giles said formally, "and you don't have to have us here if you don't want to."

"Sure." Gloria smiled bitterly. "I throw you out and you run to Quinn and tell her I'm uncooperative. Okay, question me. It won't help you find the murderer, but go ahead."

"Murderer?" Isabel asked. "You think Kruger was murdered?"

"No, I think he slipped on a banana peel and you're here to ask me if I ordered any bananas last night because Agnes, the spy, lost her notebook. Okay, I didn't eat any bananas. You can leave now, if you want to."

"I'm really interested," Giles said, "in why you think Kruger was murdered."

"You want confirmation of your logic?" Gloria was amused. "Okay, I'm working on the problem with my door locked, a chair under the doorknob, and the telephone in easy reach—I know my relatives better than you do, and that includes Victoria and Eileen—so what was Albert doing, wandering around up there in the middle of the night? Sleepwalking? Or is he making a deal for eighteen million with Victoria, Eileen, or Richard?"

"You're sure he was up there," Isabel asked, "and it was midnight? Did you see him?"

"It figures. We're not supposed to bother any of the servants after ten, but things like that don't stop on the second. If I wanted to walk around here in privacy, I'd wait until eleven, at least. Theoretically, we're not confined to our rooms between ten P.M. and seven A.M., but where do we

135

go? Fifth floor and ground floor are for servants; masters not allowed. Second floor is you and your gang. Theoretically, we can use the living room and the dining room, but to get down there, you'd be seen by the guard at the front door."

"What makes you think I have a guard at the door?" Giles asked. "Have you ever gone downstairs at night?"

"Common sense, Mr. Sullivan; give me credit. So," Gloria continued, "if you want a quiet little chat in private, it has to be either in your room or in the somebody's room. Anybody with any brains isn't going to go into Kruger's room to talk business, especially if you might decide not to go along with his brilliant schemes. You might get out alive, but your notes wouldn't. Or he might even decide to call the Dragon Lady and tell her to disqualify you because you forced your way into his room by promising sex, which is not a cause for disqualification, but once you were inside, you propositioned him to collaborate on the puzzle, which is a cause for disqualification. So, as I said, if you got such a terrific deal for me, Kruger, you come to *my* room and you bring *your* notes."

"Is that what happened?"

"Oh, sure. He called me up and offered to show me something I had never seen before, and I was so eager to get rid of my virginity that I begged him to hurry on up. But the rat fooled me. Instead of passionate kissing, he offered to show me his if I showed him mine. Puzzle notes, I mean. Well, these days a lady doesn't have to stand for rejection, so I threw him down the stairs."

"How did you know he was thrown down the stairs, Raffa?" Isabel asked.

"Because I got curious why I was in room detention, because my door can be opened a little even if I'm not allowed out, and because cops don't whisper."

"Now that you've had your fun, Raffa, why did you say he went upstairs? Couldn't he have offered the same deal to any one of you?"

"Come on, lady. If you needed to know something, who would you go to? If you needed the name of a street in the capital of Lower Slobbovia, you'd go to Sondra. If it was general braininess, you'd come to me. I know it wasn't me, and you can do an awful lot of looking through encyclopedias without risking being disqualified by Lila Quinn, so only a damn fool would go to Sondra for help. Therefore, he went up to the fourth floor."

"Victoria, Eileen, or Richard?"

"Would you go to either of the kids for *anything*? It had to be Victoria, for obscure family information."

"How could she have killed him? She can't even hold a pencil?"

"He wasn't killed with a pencil. There's nothing wrong with her feet, is there? A swift kick..."

"I think *you're* the logical choice, Raffa," Isabel said.

"If I taught you how to use makeup properly, Miss Macintosh, you wouldn't have to be so jealous." Isabel started to get up, but Giles put his hand in front of her. She was amazed, after all these years, how strong he was. And how touchy she had become about any criticism, even implied, of her sex life. "Relax, Macintosh," Gloria said, unmoved. "You started; now we're even. Look at it this way. I can see why Albert would want to team up with me. But why should I team up with him? I'm twice as smart as he is, and twice as fast. What do I gain that's worth the risk of being disqualified if we're caught?"

"Cornelius van Broek probably had an IQ that was only a little above average," Giles said, "but he's baffled a group of very intelligent people for three days, so far. Isn't it possible that Kruger found something, an approach, that none of the rest of you thought of?"

"Anything's possible, Mr. Sullivan, but it's not very likely. What approach? You think this message is hidden under seventeen layers of camouflage? Forget it; that wasn't Grandpa's style. It's in plain sight, right in front of our eyes, if we knew how to look in the right way. If Albert had the right approach, he had the whole secret message and didn't need to tie up with anybody else."

"Maybe he had the message, but didn't understand it," Isabel said.

"I wish it was that; it would mean he had to go to Aunt Vickie for sure, but it can't be. Whatever faults he had, Grandpa was a practical man. He set up this inheritance for his grandchildren and his great-grandchildren. Us, except for Aunt Vickie. He wouldn't put something in the secret message that, when we found it, we couldn't understand. It would be something that anybody, fifty years later, would understand easily, immediately, and could not misunderstand."

"Then what did Kruger offer to whomever he went to see, to induce his killer to work with him?"

"What does any man offer a girl? Promises, hot air, and bullshit, wrapped in a red ribbon and perfumed. Albert is a salesman, a real con artist, one of the best. Whoever he picked for his mark, he told her that he had a terrific lead and if she had a matching idea, they could make beautiful music together and eighteen million as well. I know," she said bitterly, "I used to fall for that crap regularly, before I got older and smarter. But some people never learn."

"You said 'she,'" Giles pointed out. "Still think it was one of the women?"

"Four to one; those are the odds."

"Which one? Really?"

"Sondra. She could make herself believe anything, if it would get a man into her bedroom. Even an Albert."

33

"**H**OW CAN YOU POSSIBLY BELIEVE HER?" ISABEL ASKED, leading Giles down the stairs. "She's an agent, an agent for movies and TV. As phony as actors and producers are, she has to be ten times as bad. I wouldn't believe her if she said, 'Good morning.'"

"It's not a question of belief, Isabel," Giles replied. "Everything she said fits what we know. Where are you leading me?"

"Away from the third floor; you heard what she said about listening at the door. Besides, I want to wash my hands; that woman gives me the creeps. The way she paints herself, during the day."

"It's probably a business requirement, Isabel. If she looked old and weak, the people she deals with would tear her to pieces."

"Old? She's six years younger than I am. She isn't even fifty."

"She doesn't exercise like you do, Isabel, or hike outdoors. I'm sure she hasn't seen a sunrise in thirty years. And she doesn't have your natural beauty."

"My natural beauty? Oh, Giles, do you really think so?"

"Well of course, Isabel. You look very fresh and wholesome."

"Fresh? Wholesome? That's another chance you missed, Sullivan."

"Missed? But I just said—"

"I know what you said, Sullivan." She sighed. "Okay, let's get back to the murder. Do you think Kruger went to Raffa's room last night?"

"She is right about one thing. If Kruger wanted to consult with the sharpest one, Gloria Raffa would be my choice, too."

"But would she let him in? Did you believe her when she said she wouldn't let anyone in?"

"I don't believe any one of them when it comes to motive, means, or opportunity. On the other hand, what could he possibly say to her that would induce her to unlock her door?"

"Maybe, Giles, maybe what he said to her had nothing to do with the puzzle. I'll bet she's just as lonely as most women her age."

"Don't be silly, Isabel. Most women her age are married."

"Exactly, Giles."

"Besides, she's in a field where she meets hundreds of attractive men."

"Sure, men who are in that field for exactly that reason. Now tell me about all the wonderful, successful men she meets: producers, directors, executives . . . Then you can tell me about all the wonderful, successful men I meet: trustees, directors, donors, accountants, lawyers . . ."

"I'm a lawyer, Isabel."

"Will you please stop changing the subject, Giles? Try to keep your mind on the murder. Who did Kruger visit, if anyone, on the fourth floor?"

"I think Gloria was right; the only reason to visit Victoria was to find out about family matters, but it is extremely doubtful that Cornelius would have had some obscure family fact as the key to the secret message. I also believe that Gloria is too smart to have let Kruger con her into believing that he had partially broken the code. So if he did visit someone on the fourth floor it had to be Eileen or Richard."

"Did it ever occur to you, Sullivan, that you have a tendency to believe the last person you spoke to, especially if she's a beautiful woman who is not the least bit fresh and wholesome?"

"I have a very sharp analytical mind, Isabel; ask any of my colleagues. Or any district attorney."

"Sure, when you're thinking. It's the other times I'm worried about."

"Isabel, you haven't been yourself these past few days. I have a feeling something is troubling you."

"The sharp analytical mind strikes again. How ever did you notice, Sullivan?"

"The way you've been acting these past few days."

"Touché. And I thought I'd been cleverly hiding it. Look, Sullivan, forget about how you ruined my plans. I have to be back at Windham early Wednesday morning. I'll make a deal with you. Clean up this whole mess, the murder and the inheritance, by Monday night, and we'll have all of Tuesday together, as a real vacation. You're not much fun when you're sleuthing and lawyering, you know. And I'm not either, I'm sure."

"And if I can't, Isabel, by then? That's only two days away. Today's Saturday, and it's almost half over."

"Then drop the whole thing. Let the police worry about Kruger; he's nothing to you. Let Lila decide who gets the inheritance; you don't really care, do you? And if Mrs. Kruger makes trouble, let Henry Winston and the insurance companies worry. A case like that could take ten years. Okay? Please, Giles? Please?"

"I'd love to, Isabel, but I can't. It wouldn't be right."

"What you're doing to me isn't right either, Sullivan, but I shouldn't have bothered to ask. I knew what the answer would be. 'Let justice be done though the heavens fall.' Okay," she said bravely, "on to Sondra Stempel."

34

"Me?" Sondra Stempel's fat cheeks grew pale. "They accused *me*?"

"Not accused," Isabel said, "but every one of your dear relatives picked you as their first choice for First Murderer."

"That's because they hate me." Sondra narrowed her eyes as though she were already plotting retribution. "They're jealous, all of them."

"Jealous? Of what?"

Sondra didn't react to the implied insult. "Of my intellect, of course. They're afraid I'll be the first to find the secret message and get all the money."

"All the more reason, Stempel, for believing that Kruger visited you last night."

"It's a reason for Albert to *want* to visit me," she said confidently, "but not for me to let him. Why should I?"

"Because he hit on an approach to the solution nobody else had thought of."

"Albert? He was the least intelligent of us all. Even Victoria is smarter than he is. Was."

"Intelligence is not the question, Stempel," Isabel pressed on. "Was Cornelius van Broek exceptionally intelligent, formally educated, well read? As I understand it, he was clever, shrewd even, but far from an intellectual. He gained his ends by a combination of hard work and concentration on one thing at a time, rather than brilliance. Look at the puzzles he constructed, as an example. They're sound, stolid, and dull; typical of their day. What he had—maybe it took an Albert Kruger to see the obvious, that all you high IQ people overlooked."

"Then why ask for my help? If I had a good approach to the solution, I would have worked on it until I had it solved. I'd never share with somebody else."

"Maybe he couldn't get anywhere with what he had, Stempel, and needed the aid of a more powerful intellect. Or maybe what he found was so obvious that he was afraid someone else would stumble on it and be able to carry it all the way to a solution. So he made a deal with you: find the solution *quickly* and the two of you split the inheritance. Nine million each is a lot better than nothing."

"If that's what happened, I would have been perfectly happy with nine million, Miss Macintosh, so why should I kill Albert?"

"Self-defense, Miss Stempel." Giles stepped in. "Precautionary self-defense. You knew Albert Kruger. You knew that the moment you found the solution, your days were numbered. Hours, more likely."

"That's silly, Mr. Sullivan." Sondra's face was flushed. She pushed a strand of hair out of her eyes. "If nine million was enough for Albert, why should he even think of killing me?"

"To make sure he got the nine million, Miss Stempel. Once you had found the solution, you could announce it yourself, and he'd be helpless to get one penny. Even killing you then wouldn't get him anything."

"That would never happen. If you knew Albert ... He was the kind of man who would have everything tied up in a contract. If *someone* double-crossed him so he couldn't get the money, he'd be in a position to make sure the other person wouldn't get it either."

"So if you killed him, Miss Stempel, and took the contract off his dead body, you'd get all the money yourself, safely."

"Why should I take all that risk if I have nine million locked up already? You're fishing, Mr. Sullivan, and your reasoning is very weak. It's clear to me that what you're saying is based on nothing but jealous gossip."

Isabel motioned Giles not to respond, that she would take over the questioning. "It just struck me, Stempel," Isabel said, "that maybe we're attacking this problem backward. Maybe Kruger didn't call you, maybe you called him to come to your room."

"I called him? Why should I? And if I did, why should he come?"

"Maybe you told him you had discovered a promising approach and needed his specialized knowledge."

"But that's ridiculous. If I had found a promising approach, why would I need him?"

"That's one way to get a man into your room."

Sondra stood up, her face contorted. Isabel remained seated and said, roughly, "Go ahead, Stempel; try it. I'm just in the mood."

Sondra sat down and began crying into her handkerchief. Isabel attacked. "When was the last time you had a man, Stempel? Or even a date? Did you ever? You tricked Kruger into coming into your room, wore your sexy black nightgown, and when he refused you, threatened to tell Quinn on you, you followed him out and pushed him downstairs."

"I didn't," she sobbed. "I didn't."

"Then you went downstairs, took his notes, and twisted his neck to make sure he was dead. You're strong enough for that. You wanted to make sure he wouldn't talk or, worse, tell Mrs. Quinn that you had tried to seduce him into collaborating with you."

"It's a lie," Sondra said, between sobs. "I never did. I really didn't."

"Why don't you confess, Stempel? Get it off your chest. You'll feel better afterward."

"I didn't do it." Sondra had stopped crying. "You're making it all up. It never happened. You have no proof; you can't have."

"When the police are finished investigating, Stempel, they'll have all the evidence they need. You murdered Albert Kruger, stole his notes, and now you're going to claim you uncovered the hidden message yourself."

"If I had done all that, Miss Macintosh, why haven't I claimed the inheritance already?"

"You're just waiting until the excitement dies down. You're afraid that if you present the solution too soon after Kruger's death, the police will tie you into the murder."

"If I had the solution, I'd be a fool to wait. Knowing the message does not tie me into any murder. Even if I killed Albert, I could show you how I figured out the message myself." Sondra was not in complete control of herself. "Your clumsy tactics may work on Richard or Eileen, but they won't work on me. Now get out, both of you. You're upsetting me and interfering with my analysis. I'm going to register a complaint against you with Mrs. Quinn."

35

"**Y**OU REALLY WENT OVERBOARD ON SONDRA STEMPEL."
Giles said, as they walked slowly downstairs. "Are you that
sure, Isabel, absolutely sure that she's the murderer?"

"I'm not sure of anything anymore, Giles; I just got fed
up. I've had it with these phonies, with the murder, with the
puzzle, the whole situation. I thought the tough approach
would work; no more Ms. Nice Guy."

"It was deliberate, then?"

"It started out that way, but when I got into the swing of
it, it felt right, so I didn't hold back."

"She was really shaken by your attack on her sex life, or
rather, the lack of it."

"Yeah, I figured she'd be most vulnerable there and I
could destroy her air of smug superiority." And I feel thoroughly ashamed of myself, Isabel thought; who am I to sneer
at another woman's needs or how she tries to satisfy them?
I'm just as assailable in that area as she is, if not more so.
And why should I assume that a woman's worth is measured
by the amount of sexual activity she grosses? In any way?
"But unfortunately, Giles, she recovered fast, and we didn't
learn anything useful."

"We learned that she's just as smart and just as tough as
Gloria Raffa."

"We've also learned that we still have five prime suspects.
The whole afternoon wasted. For what?"

"Cheer up, Isabel. Maybe one of them will panic and do
something that will give him away. Or her."

Or me, Isabel thought. I'm not as strong as you think I
am, Giles; I'm a lot closer to blowing my top than any of
those five. I'm losing control; acting in ways I don't recognize: irritable, obsessed, frustrated, and being generally
shrill and nasty. If I don't change, and fast, I may even lose

145

Giles. I don't see how he can stand me, this way; I can barely stand myself, and I don't know how to stop. Help me, Giles; can't you see what I don't dare show you? Catch the killer, find the hidden message, or drop the whole thing— to hell with the consequences—but whatever you do, do it *now*. I don't think I can hold out till Wednesday.

36

"**P**ERCIVAL CALLED," LILA REPORTED, BUSYING HERSELF with the little electric kettle on the work table. "I'll have hot chocolate ready in a couple of minutes. Tea okay for you, Giles, or do you want coffee?"

"Tea is just fine," Giles said. "Your idea or Oliver's?"

"To hell with the credits," Isabel said. "What did Percival say?"

"I'll make yours double strength," Lila said, "or would you like it injected directly? What's with you today, Isabel?"

"Nothing, Lila. Sorry." She flopped down on the couch. "Everything. I don't know. I *do* know. We've gotten exactly nowhere. Nothing is going right. Do you have *any* good news? Of any kind? I need some, desperately."

"I don't know if it's good or bad, but Percival said that Albert Kruger officially died of a broken neck. Although his arteries were fairly well clogged, there is no reason to believe he had a heart attack, or even an arterial spasm, just prior to his death. No drugs were found in his body other than aspirin and Naprosyn in normal dosage concentrations. There were no signs of ingestion or inhalation of any foreign substance, and no broken skin or contusions that are inconsistent with his falling down a carpeted stair and immediately breaking his neck. He had some arthritic calcification in his legs, hips, and shoulders, plus bursitis at the joint of his right femur with the pelvis."

"In other words," Giles summed up, "accidental death."

"Lieutenant Faber didn't come to that conclusion officially yet. Percival said that he and Faber both believed it was murder, that someone pushed him downstairs. Faber is going to sit on this till Monday. With all the running around you're doing, I think you've lost track of time, Giles. It is now Saturday afternoon, ten after three. The murder was discovered *this* morning, seven o'clock. Eight hours ago, Giles, that's all. Here's your tea. And your hot chocolate,

147

Isabel. Gulp it down. It's okay, you're among friends. I'll start another cup now."

"Eight hours?" Isabel was amazed. "That's all? My God, so it is. No wonder I'm such a nervous wreck. See, Giles? I'm not going crazy. It's just that we've packed so much into today, into half a day, that my circuits are overloaded. Isn't that second cup ready yet, Lila? And no cookies?"

"Of course, cookies; I forgot to put them out." Lila opened the desk drawer. "Here. Chocolate chip, natch. The water will be hot in another minute. You're sure you didn't pick up any clues, Giles? Give it to me word for word, while Isabel relaxes. Maybe I'll see something you missed."

"You're right, Giles," Lila said when he had finished his recital. "Nothing we hadn't already considered. Every one of them had a motive to push Kruger downstairs, plus means and opportunity, even Victoria. No witnesses, no clues, no physical evidence, and we can't even prove it was murder."

"We're not even *sure* it was murder," Giles amended.

"*You're* not sure," Lila replied. "By me, it's absolutely positively murder. Have you ever known me to be wrong when I knew something right away?"

"Not so far, Lila, but there could be a first time."

"With my logic, yes. With my positively knowing, no."

"How do we know there weren't any witnesses?" Isabel asked from the couch, noticeably relaxed. "If, say, Sondra Stempel saw Gloria Raffa pushing Albert down the stairs, why should she go to the cops?"

"Because of the odds of her winning the inheritance," Giles said, "would go to one in four."

"Isabel's right," Lila said. "If Sondra doesn't turn Gloria in, then she can blackmail Gloria for at least half the dough, maybe more. That gives Sondra odds of two in five, which is much better than one in four. Even if there's less dough, nine million is better than nothing."

"It's not all that good," Giles pointed out. "Sondra can't turn Gloria in without admitting she withheld material evidence from the police."

"It's not really a problem," Lila said. "First of all, she still has a chance of winning everything, in which case she doesn't have to bother about Gloria. And if Gloria doesn't win either, Sondra can still tap her for a few goodies for the rest of her life. And if she wants to turn Gloria in, even if she couldn't make a deal with the DA, the penalty for with-holding evidence is nothing compared to first-degree murder. She has no problem. We have the problem: even if there was a witness, no one's going to admit it."

"Can't we forget about the murder for a while?" Isabel asked. "I'm so tired of the murder I can't think straight any more. Did you get anywhere with the secret message while we were out?"

"Not a flash, Isabel; not even a flicker. And I'm tired of the damned puzzle. Every approach I tried fizzled out. I need a new approach."

"I once took a course," Isabel said thoughtfully, "many years ago, undergraduate, in problem solving. One of the techniques—I wish I could remember the author of the book, he was an engineer. It was right after we worked on the *I Ching*, the Chinese book of divination. The book is full of sayings, aphorisms, advisories. You pick three of these by some random means, by casting yarrow sticks, tossing dies, throwing coins—it doesn't matter which. You put together these three sayings and they tell you what to do to solve your problem."

"I know what it is," Lila said. "A lady on my floor lives by it. She won't go to the toilet without checking the book. She looks normal, but she's good and crazy."

"She may be, Lila, but the method can be very useful. The sayings are very vague. You take any three and you can put them together to tell you almost anything. The underlying idea is—not to a true believer, but this is the way I see it—the idea is, most people know what their problems are and what has to be done about them. But they don't act on what they know; they turn to authority or the advice of others, or they follow known paths even if these clearly lead to nowhere. Worst of all, they refuse to consider new ideas, new ways of looking at old things."

"I get it. The *I Ching* works as a way to present new ideas, or new *arrangements* of ideas, in a way which seems to be old. So your new solution gels around the combination of the three sayings. It's one you already knew subcon-sciously but didn't think of, or didn't want to think of."

"It also can stimulate a new approach. I worked out, then, that you could accomplish something similiar by opening a book at random, picking three words, and using these to focus your mind on something new."

"It worked, Isabel?"

"I tried it on several minor problems; it worked very well. Even one major problem. Kept me from marrying the wrong man. I guess I always knew it, but I didn't know I knew it, if you know what I mean."

"Of course I know. And this engineer, he worked out another way to do this?"

"Not quite. What I was leading up to—he had another way to solve problems that also focused your mind on what you knew but didn't know that you knew. He had a list of answers, a relatively short list, but you could add to it if you thought of any more good answers."

"Answers?" Giles looked at her sideways. "To problems? Like 'twenty-three' or 'see a psychiatrist'? Here's your answer, what's your question?"

"Nothing that definite, Giles. These were like—I remember one of the solutions he gave: 'To unstick, stick to something else.' You could use that as an answer for a wide variety of problems. To get rid of a persistent lover, introduce him to another girl. To get oil out of steam, use coated filters that oil sticks to. To skim fat off soup, use a brush made of oil-absorbing plastic. To get lint off a suit, use a sticky roller. Like that. You looked down the list, picked a solution that seemed applicable, and applied it to your problem. It worked very well, most of the time, and very quickly."

"And you want to use this technique," Lila asked skeptically, "to solve the crossword problem?"

"The message problem." Isabel was excited. "Just—Agatha Parrot, my secretary and a few hundred other things, has a sign on the wall behind her desk. It says, 'When all else fails, read the directions.' It's as useful for faculty as it is for students. Whenever someone comes in to complain that something isn't working the way they think it should, Agatha points to the sign. Would you believe almost half the complainers walk away right then and there? Saves a lot of wear and tear on my nerves."

"What are you getting at, Isabel?" Giles asked. "Are you suggesting that the secret message is hidden in the will itself, not the crosswords?"

"No, not that. What I'd like to try—Read me the part of the will—no, no, don't recite it to me as you remember it—*read* it to me. The part where it says how to find the hidden message."

Giles went to the safe and took out the copy of the will. He leafed through it until he found the right place. In a formal voice, he read: "...a series of crossword puzzles which, when solved, will provide the message which leads to the inheritance. When you have all the words written down, the key will appear."

"Yes, that's the part, Giles. Was that written by a lawyer?"

"By Arnold Winston? No, it's not the way he would... He was a legal scholar; very precise in his language. In fact, I doubt if these are the lawyer's words at all."

"Cornelius van Broek? Himself?"

"Almost certain, Isabel. I can't imagine Mr. Winston allowing any other layman to supply the language for van Broek's will. In fact, I can't imagine that Arnold Winston would normally have allowed Cornelius to put the directions in exactly those words; there is some ambiguity there. Van Broek must have insisted on this."

"Exactly my point. Old Cornelius wanted one of his descendants to inherit, but he wanted that one to be the most like himself. Someone who would concentrate on the problem until it was solved, who would carefully examine all aspects of the problem, who would understand his words precisely, and who was shrewd, but not necessarily well educated. And he would not leave this to chance. He would give clear directions."

"But we followed the directions exactly," Giles insisted. "All of us."

"Have we written down all the words, Giles?"

"Of course we have. Over and over."

"No we haven't," Lila said decisively. "We didn't write all the words down. We wrote all of them down, but we didn't write them *down*. We just wrote the Down words down." She opened the drawer and took out the three solved puzzles. Selecting Puzzle Number One, she started writing:

```
BBAANMKIBEORLXBEOENCEOOSNSECEAGIPGCHFTN
ARLLOEENAXREOAALNMAHVMAPOHLONRANOIOAORO
RUPAIANNNTAEGVEISUGOIOTIRIFAAAMCLBRTRED
 T SSTTEEOND IDE  SSL  LMN TMMBUEEDE E
   Y  R RG  EEL   E   EAE  EA R  S
         TE  RK           ND  LE
         E   E           E    N
         D   R           Y
```

They studied the pattern for several minutes. "I don't see a thing," Lila said. "You. Giles?"

"No," Giles said, regretfully. "Isabel?"

"Maybe that's not down enough," Isabel said. "How about putting one word under the next?"

"My paper isn't long enough," Lila said. "I'll write it horizontally; should be exactly the same."

BARBRUTALPALASNOISYMEATKENTINNERBANE
EXTORTEDORANGEREEDLOGXAVIERBAEDEKER
ELIELONSEMUNAGSCHOSEEVILOMOOATSPILE
NORMANDYSHINEDELFCOATENAMELARAMAEN
GAMBINCURPOLEGIBECORDSHATEFORTREENOD

Giles picked up his pencil, but did not write, "Sorry, Isabel, this isn't it."

"Why not, Giles? There could easily be a code in there."

"There could be ten codes in there, but it's not right. It would take an expert cryptanalyst to pull a clear message out of this; there's nothing obvious that I can see. It's not the way Cornelius worked. He wouldn't require that his heir be a cryptanalyst."

There was dead silence as the three of them stared helplessly at the paper on the table. Then Isabel cried, "We're writing it down wrong. Write the Across words across, but put them down, one under the other."

"That's it," Lila shrieked. "An acrostic. I *know* that's it." She immediately started writing.

BAR
BRUT
ALP
ALAS
NOISY
MEAT
KENT
INNER
BANE
EXTORTED
ORANGE
REED

LOG
XAVIER
BAEDEKER
ELIEL
ONS
EMU
NAGS
CHOSE
EVIL
OMO
OAT
SPILE
NORMANDY
SHINED
ELF
COAT
ENAMEL
ARAMAEN
GAMB
INCUR
POLE
GIBE
CORDS
HATE
FOR
TREE
NOD

"Oh, my God," Isabel said, deflated, "there's nothing there either. Well, I tried."

"Shut up, Isabel," Lila said. "It's there. I know it. I said it's there and it *is* there. Just let me think."

"Every other word?" Isabel brightened up. "The first letter of every other word. Look: B-A-N-K. Start writing, Lila." She dictated slowly. "'BANKBOLBONEONEEGPCFN.' No, that's not it; there's something wrong."

"No there isn't," Giles said. "That's it. There are three words in there, BANK, BONE, and ONE. That's too many for coincidence." He studied the line of letters. "No, it can't be a transposition," he muttered to himself, "it smells wrong. And it isn't a substitution, I'm sure of that." He studied the letters a full minute. "Let me have the filled-out puzzle."

Lila handed him the puzzle. Giles studied it, looking from the puzzle to the line of letters, then back again, again and again, back and forth. Then his intent face relaxed. "Yes, that's it. Simple. Really simple." He smiled, for the first time in four days. "Here's the rule. Write the Across words down to form an acrostic. Take the first letter of each alternate word *but*, when the first letter of a word *in the puzzle diagram* is directly under a first letter that's already been used, go to the next word, and keep going. Just so you don't have two acrostic letters next to each other in the diagram. So simple, once you know how. That's all there is to it. So 'B-A-N-K-B-O' is correct. But the next alternate letter 'L' is directly under the 'O' in 'ORANGE,' which has been used before, so we go to the first letter of the next word, 'X,' in 'XAVIER.' This gives us 'BANK BOX ONE ONE EIGHT.'"

"That's it," Lila said, satisfied. "I knew it was there." She put Puzzle Number Two in front of her. "I'll do this myself. 'KEY TEN COMDMTS SCOUT.' Perfect. He just left out a few letters. It reads, 'KEY TEN COMMAND-MENTS, SCOUT.' I know what has to come next, but let's check Puzzle Number Three. 'LAWS BILL OF RIGHTS.' Now to put the whole thing together: 'BANK BOX ONE ONE EIGHT. KEY: TEN COMMANDMENTS, SCOUT LAWS, BILL OF RIGHTS.' The Ten Commandments, the Boy Scout Laws, and the Bill of Rights. Wasn't the alternate heir the Boy Scouts of America, Giles?"

"They're the ones. That's another clue van Broek gave, so that when the heir got the message, he'd be sure he was right."

"It's a pity we can't collect, Giles," Lila said. "Are you sure, Isabel, you're not a direct descendant of Cornelius van Broek? I know I'm not, and I could really use six million dollars."

"No, Lila, sorry. Scotch descent all the way back. But I don't care; I'm just happy it's over. Now we can all relax."

"We can't, Isabel," Giles said. "It's great we did it, thanks to you, but now we have to be doubly careful. We can't let this get out, not even that we've found the hidden message. Lila, shred all the papers and flush them down the toilet. Your notes too, everything. From now on, we have to watch everything we say, even in private. Neither by word nor by gesture, as the saying goes, can we let any of the heirs know that we know what we know."

"One of them may know already, Giles," Lila said.

"How? No, that's impossible. If any of them—"

"It's not the message that they have to find; it's the money they have to get. The money is in box one eighteen, the bank has to be the one van Broek originally put his money in, the trustee of the estate. The winner has to go there, ask for box one eighteen, and say, or write, 'Ten Commandments, Scout Laws, Bill of Rights,' in front of the vice-president of the trust division. Then the vice-president has to unseal the envelope in the box and see if the message matches. *Then* the winner gets the eighteen million dollars in the form of a bank check made out to him then and there. No digging, he just starts an account in his own name."

"But what has that to do with...?" Isabel asked.

"It's Saturday," Lila said. "The bank is closed. If one of them found the secret message, she, or he, better keep her big mouth shut until she goes to the bank at nine A.M. Monday morning, with Giles and Oliver as bodyguards and witnesses. Otherwise we might find another body which accidentally fell down the stairs."

"Oh, God." Isabel put her head into her hands. "It's starting all over again."

37

"It seems to me," Oliver said, after refilling the little electric kettle and plugging it in again, "that we are no closer to solving any of the previous problems than we were before." He had brought two boxes of chocolate-chip cookies and arranged them on two plates; one he placed on the study table between Lila and Giles, the other he set in front of Isabel.

"But we did find the secret message," Lila stated.

"Very commendable, madam, but this now requires supreme acting ability on the part of all of us, so as not to alert the killer. If he, or as you keep insisting she, has the slightest idea that one of us has the secret message, she will assume that all of us have it. It is very difficult to guard four people against five potential killers, especially since they do not have the problem of gaining entry into these premises."

"What would she gain if she killed us?"

"The death of one of us, Miss Isabel, might be a warning not to interfere with the killer's schemes."

"But when the killer claimed the inheritance, we'd know who she is."

"The killer might not believe that we would seek retribution. Or if he did, he might decide to insure that we could not."

Isabel shuddered. "Kill five people?"

"For eighteen million dollars? If you will perform the indicated arithmetic, madam, you will find the reward per murder is well above market."

"The police would be suspicious. She'd never get away with it."

"The police require proof, madam, before arresting a millionaire. However, I do not believe it will happen that way."

"That's good, Oliver. Or is it?"

156

"Nothing in this situation can be good, madam. If I were the murderer, I would entice, or kidnap, one of you and apply appropriate tortures until you divulged the secret message. Then I would kill you, no matter how earnestly you swore you would not tell. Push you down the stairs, bound and gagged, for instance, then run down, break your neck, and remove the bindings."

"But wouldn't that leave marks?"

"Elastic Ace bandages, applied for a short time, do not leave marks."

"But then, no matter what happens, all four of us are slated for murder."

"So it appears, madam, in any probable scenario."

"You seem to know a great deal about this, Oliver," Lila said.

"Yes, madam; I read a good many whodunits."

"But isn't there any way out of this?" Isabel asked.

"There is always a way out, madam. We can all act as though we have had no success in finding the secret message."

"Not me," Lila said. "I can't even keep a secret from my grandchildren. One look at my face and she'd know."

"I might be able to keep it quiet for a day," Isabel said, "but I don't know how long I'd be able to keep it up. One thing for sure, I'm not going into anyone's room alone."

"I'm sure you would not, madam, but if Mr. Giles were to receive a frantic call in the middle of the night, what would he do?"

"He'd grab his sword cane and run," Isabel said ruefully. "And make sure not to wake me."

"Further, the attack might not take place in anyone's room. As the insurance companies advertise, most accidents take place in the home, but in areas other than the bedroom. No area is safe, and if we made it a point not to be alone with any of our guests, what we are doing would soon become evident. The killer would then understand why, and might be moved to take quicker action."

"Isn't it possible that the killer already has the solution?" Lila asked. "After all, didn't we assume that she let Kruger into her room because he had a promising approach?"

"That was one of the possibilities we examined," Isabel said. "I wish it were true."

"Then why don't we make sure?" Lila asked. "I really don't care who gets the money, as long as I don't. Let's give the killer the solution. That way, we'd all be safe."

"The question is, madam, who is the killer?"

"What's the difference?" Lila asked. "Give the sentence to each one, secretly, and let them all kill each other."

"Would you encourage murder?" Giles was shocked.

"Better them than me, Giles. Or any of us."

"No, I can't allow that. There must be a better way."

"Sure, Giles. Get the killer before he gets me."

"Yes," Giles said. "Of course. Why didn't I think of it? Everybody out. Go to your own rooms. Don't bother me. I'll call you when I'm finished." He rummaged in the table drawer.

As they left, Lila said to Isabel. "What's he doing?"

"Constructing a crossword."

"At a time like this?"

"It's to catch the killer."

"He knows who it is?"

"Of course. That's why he's constructing the puzzle. He's done it before. In Vermont," Isabel added.

"So why doesn't he tell us?"

"He likes to be mysterious. He's a big show-off."

"Do you know who the killer is?"

"Not the slightest idea. Do you?"

"No flash. Not even one candlepower. He'll tell us, won't he?"

"Of course. When he finishes constructing the puzzle."

Lila sighed. "Isn't it too bad we don't have Hannibal handy?"

"Yes," Isabel said. "It is too bad."

ACROSS

1 "Woe ___!"
5 Invoice stamp
9 Chowderhead, for short
13 Tourney type
14 "...calm, ___ bright"
16 Bookshelf burden
17 Would like to have
18 Saw pieces
19 Luke's adviser
20 Various and sundry
22 It follows 12, but not 13
24 Larry's cohort
25 *Tête* that wears a crown?
26 Moderate brown
28 They have a lot of pluck
33 Distorted
34 Peter or Franco
36 Without a clear winner
37 Mischief Night missiles
39 Lack of perpendicularity
41 Barn adjunct

42 —*être* (maybe): Fr.
43 Family friends
44 Equal-rights movement,
   for short
45 Having a fit?
48 "Hello, ___ Be Going"
51 Not Lib. or Cons.
52 Nancy's man
53 Major mental anguish
56 Gizmo for a kid whose
   parents work
61 Wallow
62 Short-billed rail
64 Destroy
65 "___ Ben Adhem"
66 "Lady" in a 1932 song
67 Spots before one's eyes?
68 Cribbage necessities
69 Sunday morn rendition
70 Lane's coworker

DOWN

1 River to the Mississippi
2 Bad Ems and Baden-
   Baden
3 ___ sana in corpore sano
4 Bury
5 Symmetric arrangements
6 Out of the storm
7 "___ Three Lives"
8 Morse morsel
9 Conforms to 5 Down
10 Grand total?
11 Eight CCCXXVs
12 Mountaineer's goal
15 Chevrolet sponsored her
   TV show
21 Old-time baseballer
   "Preacher"
23 Miler Sebastian
26 One who gives incentive
27 1964 Mary Wells hit song
28 Prepare for a bout
29 Absolutely refuses to

30 "The ___ that men do ..."
31 Changed the bulb, maybe
32 Holier-than-thou type,
   perhaps
33 "Jesus ___": John 11:35
35 Nevada city
38 Spur
40 Last Supper quorum
46 Pierre or Philippe, e.g.
47 American princess
49 Indian shoe, for short
50 Shuck the corn
53 Hunter's purchase
54 Judicial cover
55 Like falling off ___
56 Tramp's love
57 Actor Tamiroff
58 Baby's seat, maybe
59 Flawless location
60 Eddie of baseball lore
63 Gallery's cry

Puzzle No. 4

IN LESS THAN TWO HOURS, GILES CALLED THEM ALL BACK in. He had a copy of his crossword in place for Oliver, as well as for Lila and Isabel. "Try it," he said, "Tell me if there are any problems."

"That was pretty fast, Giles," Lila said, taking out her fine-point pen and getting to work.

"I wasn't trying for any records," Giles said. "I was just trying to get a message across to the killer."

"It's a relief to get a competent puzzle for a change." Lila's pen was flying. "Cornelius van Broek had no pizzazz. Solving his puzzles was like drinking dishwater."

"You must remember, Lila, he wasn't trying to create an elegant puzzle; he was trying to hide a message. Further, his puzzles were made in the thirties; crossword-puzzle construction has come a long way in the past fifty years."

"Yeah? Well, he's still a bore. I'd hate to be married to him. Good for you, Giles, on twenty-eight Across. You're no Hannibal, but you do have your moments."

"I like forty-five Across," Isabel said. "You can be cute, if you want to, Giles."

"You're ahead of me?" Lila asked, without lifting her eyes from her puzzle. "Or did Giles fill in half of yours?"

"Don't sweat, Lila," Isabel said. "I don't always start from one Across like you do. You're still champ."

"You had me scared for a moment," Lila said. "I thought I was losing my grip. Twenty-two Across and ten Down are okay, too, Giles."

"Sixty-seven Across is nice too," Isabel said. "And fifty-eight Down, forty Down, and fifty-one Across aren't too bad."

"If you're talking *acceptable*," Lila said, "sixteen Across, thirty-seven Across, and forty-one Across are passable. The rest...? I'd give this a B minus at best, Giles."

"But is it appropriate for our contestants?" Giles asked. "In terms of difficulty?"

"Too good for those *momzers*," Lila said. "But not too hard. Maybe a spot here and there, but the crossings give them away."

"You're finished already?" Isabel squealed. "Why do I let myself do crosswords with you? It's so humiliating."

"Don't be humiliated, Isabel. It's not brains, it's a gift. Like having a second head. It's very useful at times, and it's a living, but I don't know how I do it. It's not teachable, although I do give classes that are helpful, and it's not inheritable; my kids aren't even *interested* in crosswords. I'd trade it all, Isabel, for your age and your looks, so don't be envious."

"I'm still envious, Lila. The trick with envy is not to be reasonable, but to want it all. Thanks for the compliment; it's time *somebody* around here noticed."

"The puzzle is perfectly satisfactory, sir," Oliver announced. "Just the right balance of all the elements."

"Okay, kids," Lila said, "I see we're all finished. And the message is: 'I SAW YOU WE SPLIT CASH.' Very good, Giles. I like that approach. Make the murderer sweat a little, then call the cops. I take it, I pass these out when I collect Puzzle Number Three from our five *momzers*? It's almost six o'clock. Can you get them all down here by six, Oliver?"

"I'm sure all our guests are most anxious to be allowed to leave their rooms." He left the study quickly.

"Okay, then, Isabel"—Lila became efficient—"put the solved puzzles in the drawer temporarily. Warm up the copying machine and we'll go through the routine one more time. Giles, go away. Lock yourself in your room. I don't want you around here when the crowd starts bitching about being locked up all day."

"Whatever you say, Lila; you're the judge."

"One thing, Giles. You're assuming the murderer knows the key to finding the secret message."

"Of course. I think that's a reasonable assumption."

"What if she doesn't?"

"Then there's no way to trap her," Giles said bluntly.

"She gets away with murder? Not by me, she doesn't. I want her caught, Giles, so I can sleep nights. I want you to spend the next hour figuring how to get the killer just in case she doesn't know the key. But okay, it's not that I disagree with you, Giles, I was just exploring all the possibilities. I'm ninety-nine percent sure she has to know the key. Let's go on from there. This puzzle won't take long to do. After she decodes the message, she'll have almost two hours to sweat before we meet for supper. So let's add to the pressure. Tell Ping to prepare a clumsy, sloppy meal. I don't mean badly cooked, but stuff that's hard to eat. Fruit compote with lots of pits. Broiled lobster. Stuff like that. I want the makeup smeared, the hands greasy, and each one wondering what to do with pits and shells. Two martinis before dinner; the more embarrassing their behavior, the better. And brandy afterward."

"You're asking me to *embarrass* my guests," Giles said.

"I want the murderer to give herself away in front of everybody, to break down. It's not enough that we know. You're not embarrassing your guests, I am. I'm testing them, actually; part of my job as judge. So your conscience is clear, Giles. Do it, please."

Giles started to leave. "Wear your coldest, toughest expression tonight, Giles," Lila added. "I want her to sweat blood. But don't say a word, no matter what. Not one word. Let me handle the conversation. Don't stare, either. Just play it cool, act natural. Isabel, Oliver, and I will watch the murderer." She paused expectantly. "All right. I know you're playing games, Giles, waiting for me to ask. So I'll ask: Who's the murderer?"

"Who is she?" Giles looked perplexed. "But I thought you understood. I don't have the slightest idea."

"Oh, I don't think I should take a second martini, Oliver." Victoria van Broek put her hand to her bosom. "I'm beginning to feel a bit tiddly already."

"I'm sure Mr. Sullivan would be most pleased if you would accept, madam. He realizes that you have all been greatly inconvenienced by the events of the day." He placed the cocktail on the table and removed the empty glass. Without asking, he placed a fresh martini in front of each person. When he got to Isabel, he noticed that she had not touched her drink. "Please try it, madam," he whispered. "I am sure you will be pleased." Isabel picked up the drink and sipped cautiously. It was ice cold crème de cacao. She threw the drink down her throat, picked up the second glass, and began sipping slowly, smiling at her dinner companions.

"Did you construct today's puzzle?" Gloria Raffa asked Giles.

"Of course he did," Lila said. "Can't you tell the difference?"

"It was because I could tell the difference, Mrs. Quinn, that I asked. I was just wondering why a fourth puzzle was required."

"There'll be as many puzzles as I decide," Lila said. "Since nobody found the secret message yet, I'll have to use other puzzles to help make my decision."

Steamers with drawn butter were served.

"But we still have time," Richard Deddich said, "to find the message, according to the will."

"The race is over at noon, Wednesday," Lila said. "If you find it before then, I won't have to choose between you. But if none of you gets the message by then, I want to be prepared."

"The message is in the three puzzles only?" Eileen asked. "The ones Great-Grandfather made up?"

"That's what the will said," Lila agreed.

"Then what's the use of the fourth puzzle if there's no message in it?" Eileen persisted.

"How well you handle it and how you comport yourselves will be among my considerations."

"Did you have any trouble with the fourth puzzle?" Sondra Stempel asked. "I don't see how any of us could have failed to solve it."

"I have no trouble with crosswords," Lila said. "I'm glad you think you don't. Just keep doing your best, hand it in to me, and I'll do the rest."

The sour cherry soup, au naturel, was served.

"What time must we hand it in?" Victoria asked. "I was prepared to hand in the third puzzle at noon today, but you weren't ready until six."

"Six again, tomorrow," Lila answered. "Unless some other complication arises."

"Some other complication?" Gloria arched her eyebrows. "That's a sweet way to put it."

"What did the police say?" Richard asked. "Nobody told me anything and there was nothing on the radio."

"Albert Kruger died of a broken neck," Lila said. "Caused by falling downstairs."

"When did you find this out?" Sondra asked.

The barbecued spareribs were served, accompanied by corn on the cob and asparagus hollandaise.

"Three o'clock."

"Then why was I hounded"—Sondra was indignant—"and practically accused of killing him?"

"We didn't know of the police report," Isabel said, "until after we saw you."

"Besides," Lila added, "the police just said Kruger died of a broken neck. They didn't say he wasn't pushed."

Eileen choked on her sparerib. "Please, not while I'm eating." She pushed the spareribs away and started on the asparagus.

"Murdered?" Gloria asked.

"But they have only questioned us once," Victoria said.

"They'll be back tomorrow or Monday," Lila said, "don't worry. As soon as they've checked your backgrounds and your stories against each other."

"Ours?" Gloria asked. "Not yours, too?"

"I've got nothing to gain by murdering Albert Kruger," Lila explained.

"And we do?" Gloria asked.

"Damn right," Lila said. "And don't act as if you don't know it, Raffa. I know you do, all of you, and next time the police come around, I'm going to tell them what I think: that one of you killed him."

There was dead silence, broken only by Oliver announcing that there would be stuffed artichokes instead of salad.

"I don't like your accusation," Richard said. "It's totally unwarranted."

"It's not an accusation, Deddich; it's an opinion. Which, if you bother to think about it, is totally warranted."

"I protest that, too, Mrs. Quinn," Eileen said indignantly. "You're supposed to be a judge who may end up deciding which one of us gets the inheritance and you're supposed to be impartial. I don't want you to tell the police your libellous opinions."

"You tell the police what you want; I'll tell them what I want. If the police ask me a question, I have to answer truthfully. And I am impartial. Did I say which one of you did it?"

Dessert was served. Ripe mangoes, papayas, and muscat grapes.

"You know who did it, Mrs. Quinn?" Richard asked. "If you do, you're obligated to tell us, too."

"I've got a good idea, Deddich," Lila said, with a meaningful look, "but I'm not saying anything until I have real proof. And since when am I obligated to even talk to you?"

They ate in silence. Oliver served the brandy in big snifters. They all drank all of the brandy. Victoria and Sondra held out their snifters for seconds. Oliver obliged them.

Giles stood up, and they all left the table. He signaled Lila and Isabel to remain behind. When he was sure all five of his guests were in the living room, he said quietly, "You deliberately gave them the impression that you know who the murderer is, Lila."

"Yeah," she said. "Just in case the murderer doesn't know how to read the message in your crossword."

"That could be very dangerous, Lila."

"So what other big thrills are left to me," she said fatalistically, "at my age?"

LIEUTENANT FABER SENT ME," PERCIVAL SAID, "BECAUSE he doesn't want to come here officially." He took another big slice of marble cake off the plate on the study table as Oliver refilled his coffee cup. "Until he has some evidence of murder, he wants to keep things quiet."

"I take it Mrs. Kruger is making difficulties," Giles said.

"You have no idea, but there's nothing she can do until it's officially a murder or an accident, one or the other."

"We all know it was murder," Lila said. "What's the big problem?"

"What we know, Mrs. Quinn, and what Faber signs his name to—that's two different things."

"You went through my notes, Percival," Giles said. "Did you see anything there I might have missed?"

"Not a thing. The trouble is, we're in limbo. If I could just take them downtown, one at a time, and have a little talk . . ."

"So talk to them here," Lila said. "Costs nothing."

"I can't. Faber doesn't want anything official done without his being here. I'm only here as Giles's brother, that's all. Of course, if I happen to pick up anything . . ."

"I think it would be better if you didn't talk to anyone, Percival," Isabel said. "The situation is getting ready to explode. Giles gave them a puzzle last night in which he hid a message using the same technique as the contest message. The message says he saw the killer commit the murder and he wants her to split the inheritance with him. It also shows that he knows the secret message that's worth eighteen million dollars, so the killer has to worry that Giles might let the information slip accidentally, or even make a deal with another of the relatives to cut her out completely. First one wins, so in spite of going to all that trouble to kill Kruger, the killer might end up with nothing."

"You're setting yourselves up as targets, Giles?" Percival asked. "Without knowing who the killer is?" He thought for a while. "I guess there's nothing else you could do, but you got to be real careful."

"It's not all that bad, Perce," Giles said. "There are no guns available to any of the five, nor knives. Oliver counts everything after each meal. There's no way for one of them to get into the first-floor kitchen."

"Yeah? Not even by pulling the night man away with a phony call for help? And what about the cellar kitchen? Going down by elevator?"

"I have started sleeping in the cellar kitchen," Oliver said, "since last night. My cot is across the elevator entrance. The night man is under orders to call the footman in case of emergency; he will not leave his post. In addition, the floor maids search the rooms at least once a day."

"Yeah, okay, but there's a hundred other ways to kill somebody if you really want to. Jesus, Giles, you sure got a way with making problems, don't you?"

"Don't worry, Percival; we're not dealing with professional killers. Most of the other ways involve personal contact. I make sure to keep my eyes open all the time. Besides, most of the time, Isabel is with me."

"You're putting her in danger, too? That's smart, Giles. That's real smart."

"I don't think the killer will attack two people at once," Isabel said. "I'm more worried about something else. Last night at dinner, Lila talked as though she knew who the killer was."

"Jeeesus. What were you trying to do, Quinn? Take the heat off Giles?"

Lila nodded. "And trying to confuse the killer a little, too."

"Now you're a target, too. For that matter, so are Isabel and Oliver. When it was Giles alone, I could handle it, but there's no way for me to protect the four of you. Boy, Giles, when you mess things up, you *really* mess things up. Amateurs!"

"Don't get so upset, Percival," Lila said. "This type of killer isn't going to break my door down, and there's no way I'm going to let anybody into my room when I'm alone."

"Yeah? What about when you're in this study? All day long. Alone. They got a right to come in here, you said."

"I'll keep Isabel with me."

"Before, Giles said he's keeping Isabel with him. Jeeesus; a college president for a bodyguard. So who gets the bodyguard? And what about Oliver? Any one of them could tell him to come to his room."

"Or her room," Isabel said.

"Yeah, her room. You know what I mean. Okay, there's no way out of it; I'm staying here."

"But we can't have the police here," Giles said. "It isn't officially a murder, yet. The heirs could sue us."

"I'm not the police, Giles. I'm your brother, remember? If I ain't allowed to visit, who is? Don't worry, I won't act like a cop."

"But there's no room, Percival. The servants are doubled up already."

"You got one empty room, Giles. Kruger's. Oliver can fix it up in two minutes. Okay with you, Oliver?"

"An excellent suggestion, sir. I have toilet articles and everything you will need, sir, except nightclothes in your size. Shall I send a messenger?"

"I'll pick them up myself. I'm going to Mass and confession. Want to come with me, Giles? It's Sunday, remember?"

"I'm sorry, Percival, but I haven't gone to Mass since—for eighteen years. I don't think I could go now."

"She would have wanted it, Giles. Sorry, Isabel."

"I understand, Percival," Isabel said. Giles was silent.

"Mom would have wanted it, too, Giles."

"I have too much work to do," Giles said. "The five suspects will be turning in their puzzles, Number Four, at six tonight. I have to have a puzzle ready at that time to trap the murderer, otherwise the whole effect of what I'm trying to do will fizzle."

"To trap the murderer, Giles?" Percival's face lit up. "You know who he is?"

"Of course not, that's the trouble. How could I know? If I could only think—. My head is so full . . . I don't even know where to start looking."

"Come to Mass with me," Percival said kindly. "And go to confession. Get it all off your chest. You'll feel much better. Your head will be clear, and your soul. Your conscience will be clear, too; it was never your fault, Giles, not directly. Then you'll be able to think clearly. I do it all the time. It works, Giles; believe me, it really works."

Giles put his head down, his face twisted. He didn't speak. Isabel got up and put her arms around him. Percival watched Giles, sadly, for a while, then left.

As soon as the door closed behind Percival, Isabel pulled Giles to his feet. "Go take a nap, Giles," she said. "You're all worn out with worry. I'll stay with you."

"He can't," Lila said. "He's got to construct another crossword."

"But he must have some rest," Isabel protested. "He was awake all last night."

"It's almost four o'clock, Isabel. They'll be here at six. You know how he is. If he doesn't have the puzzle ready, he'll feel even worse. I don't give a damn, personally, if we catch the murderer or not. You decide."

"Stop talking about me as though I'm not here," Giles said. "I am here. I can make my own decisions."

"So what's your decision?"

"I have to construct the crossword; it's my responsibility."

"Without a message?"

"No, there must be a message." Giles looked totally drained. "Please leave. I have to get started now."

"A message?" Lila was astounded. "You've figured out who the murderer is in the last minute?"

"Of course not. How could I?"

"Then what will the message be?"

"I don't know. Maybe the message will come to me when I start working."

Lila looked at Isabel sympathetically, took her arm, and led her to the door.

ACROSS
1 China Sea feeder
8 Muleta user
15 Sunken space near a
    basement
16 Quondam
17 G.I. John
18 Boxer Sonny, et al.
19 Hesitant interjections
20 Get all snug and cozy
22 La vache qui ___
23 Gentlemen
24 Beauty-parlor application
27 Relaxed
30 West of Hollywood
31 Senate Watergate
    Committee chairman
35 The picture of health?
36 Wave participant
37 Display of ostentation
38 C

39 Man of many parts?
41 Tu ___ pas (you are not):
    Fr.
42 Workshop machine
44 Sound of impact
45 "Meet me ___ Louis"
46 Halloween option
47 Gentile
48 Clothing-store assortment
49 More state-of-the-art
51 Fam. member
52 Quick 40
55 Plays the tattletale
57 Ant.
60 Lawmaker, at times
63 Stomp on
65 Tell the tale
66 Modern-day dunce
67 Agog
68 New Jersey port city

DOWN
1 Korea Bay feeder
2 Khachaturian
3 Trapezists' insurance
4 Needlefish
5 Interlaced
6 Author Grey, et al.
7 Sightseers?
8 Parnis of fashion
9 Green-card bearer
10 6-pt. scores
11 Bar tender: Abbr.
12 A-line developer
13 Atlanta arena
14 Whatever's left
21 Move
23 Attention getter
25 Burn a bit
26 Screw up someplace
27 Be
28 Bellowing
29 River of France
30 Answer to the Sphinx's
    riddle
32 Pat's hostess

33 That is for Caesar
34 Fits inside snugly
36 Voting favorably
37 Baptist bench?
39 Apportion
40 Stocking stuffer
43 Rather or Rowan
45 Debtor's letters
47 Ready, with "up"
48 Pet-shop buy
50 "Murder, She ___"
51 The Andrea ___
52 50th-state bird
53 "Lizzie Borden took ___"
54 Place of récréation
56 Attempt
57 Word with season or
    sesame
58 Make preparations
59 Foot: Suffix
61 Dernier ___
62 Action demanding a tit?
64 Unit of conductance

Puzzle No. 5

41

"**F**OR A GUY WHO WAS READY TO PACK IT IN LESS THAN two hours ago," Lila said, writing as she spoke, "this is a pretty neat puzzle. Thirty-five Across, thirty-nine Across, seven Down, and eleven Down are very nice. Seventeen Across, fifty-two Across, and three Down aren't bad either."

"Thirty-seven Down and sixty-two Down are *excellent*," Isabel said. "And forty-five Down and fifty-four Down are good, too. So is fifty-two Across."

"Even thirty Across, thirty-six Across, and forty-six Across are acceptable, Giles. What happened? Oliver brought you some vitamins?"

"Read the message," Giles said. "That's the important part. Tell me what you think of it."

"'YOURRMXPMSIGNNOTE,'" Lila read as she wrote. "Meaning 'I'll meet you in your room at ten P.M. whereupon you will sign a note.' That's for the money you were supposed to split with me as per Puzzle Number Four? So I won't tell the police I saw you push Kruger down the stairs?"

"Exactly. I'm glad it's clear."

"So you did have an inspiration after all," Isabel said. "I knew you could do it. Who's the killer?"

"I don't know yet. The message was my only inspiration."

Lila looked at him in amazement. "You're depending on one of them giving herself away between six and ten tonight? Lots of luck, Giles."

"You want to watch them during dinner," Isabel asked, "to see who acts nervous and irritable?"

"Yes. All three of us. Four. Oliver, too."

"How do you tell," Lila asked, "the difference between a guilty conscience and hating shark's-fin soup? Or hating me, for that matter? I don't think they like you very much either, or Isabel. Or each other."

174

"And Percival," Isabel reminded. "None of them are going to love him. In fact, when he's around, I feel like confessing to something myself, and I've led a reasonably clean life."

"The most suspicious-looking character at dinner tonight," Lila said, "is going to be you, Giles. In fact, I don't think you should be at dinner tonight at all. Let's eat here. Percival, too. Maybe, between us, we'll think of something."

"I've already prepared an alternative plan," Giles said. "If I can't determine who the killer is before ten, I'll just phone each one in turn. I'll say, 'I'm coming up now,' and see what the response is. That's why I worded the message that way."

"No good, Giles." Lila shook her head. "First of all, you're assuming that the murderer can read the message. That's not guaranteed, but it's a reasonable assumption, so I'll accept it. Now what happens if you call, say, Gloria, and say, 'I'm coming up now,' or something like that. Assuming she recognizes your voice, what do you do if she says, 'That's very flattering, but I've got a headache'?"

"Then I call the next one."

"Each one is going to respond with something that has nothing to do with blackmail or murder, or even an indication that she understood the message. If I were the murderer in this situation, I would at least make you tell me what you were coming up for and exactly what you saw. Specifically. No *phumpha*ing. And the exact time and circumstances. Everything, before I unbolted my door. And if what you said did not match exactly what I did and how I did it, and the exact time, I'd just hang up."

"All right, I won't phone. I'll just go up and knock on each door until I get the proper response."

"Anyone knocks on my door at night, I'm going to yell, 'Who is it?' and you have to tell me your name loudly and clearly enough to be heard through my door. Which means heard through every door on the floor. Maybe even one of the others opens the door a crack, keeping the chain on, and watches and listens. After Victoria refuses to let you in, you think Eileen will? And again, after she asks you who is it, she's going to say, 'What do you want?' You have an answer ready for that, one that you want to shout all over the house?"

"Then what am I do to? If I can't watch them, can't phone them, and can't go to their rooms..."

"Think. You can think. Go to your room now, the horde will be here in a few minutes. Lie down. Take a tranquilizer. Rest. Relax. Try to sleep. Something may come to you. I'll tell Oliver to serve supper here, with Percival. Bounce your ideas off us then. We'll have a brainstorming session. Something will fall out, Giles. Don't worry." Lila put her hand over her mouth apologetically. "Sorry about that, Giles. It just slipped out."

42

"**S**HOULDN'T YOU BE DOWNSTAIRS IN THE DINING ROOM right now?" Percival asked.

"Mrs. Quinn impressed on me," Oliver replied, "the importance of my presence here, sir. If there is anything I can do to help . . . ?"

"You're leaving the five suspects all alone, Oliver?"

"Not quite, sir. I've pressed the footman and the night man into attendance. The service will not be quite as good as that of the past few days, but it will have to do." He sliced and served the roast beef quickly and efficiently, and followed it with potatoes Anna and *petites pois*.

"I was expecting sandwiches," Isabel said. "It was thoughtful of you and Ping to prepare such a good meal on such short notice."

"It's the same dinner that is being served in the dining room now, madam. Very little additional effort was required."

"While I was drowsing," Giles said, "somebody told me who the murderer was, but I didn't understand. He was dressed all in gray and his face was hidden. It was in snatches. Something about irrigating the desert—that's all I remember."

"Irrigating the desert?" Lila asked. "Sounds like one of Hannibal's clues. You couldn't tell who it was?"

"I was sure I knew the voice; someone I had spoken to recently."

"Someone in this house?" Percival probed. "The murderer?"

"I have the feeling it was one of our guests. I haven't been out of the house since Wednesday. Yes," Giles said decisively, "I'm sure it was someone in this house."

"It could very well have been the murderer in your dream," Isabel said, "confessing to you, although it was actually your subconscious that had figured out who she was. Sometimes, just as I'm waking up, I have a vision of a newspaper showing me all sorts of interesting things that are going to happen. I read the paper with perfect comprehension, but when I'm fully awake, I don't remember a thing. Was it a man or a woman who spoke to you?"

"I couldn't tell, Isabel. I got the distinct impression that it was trying to be helpful, but I'll be damned if I understand what it meant."

"There was something by Byron"—Isabel wrinkled her forehead—"about irrigating the desert, but I . . . Give me a minute; it's a long time since I taught literature. It was something like—like water the desert. Yes. I have it. 'Alas! our young affections run to waste, Or water but the desert.'"

"Hey," Lila said. "Eileen. She's the youngest."

"Richard Deddich is also young," Giles said, "and Sondra Stemple is only a little older than he is. Besides, I'm not very familiar with Byron. It's doubtful that my subconscious would pick something like that."

"You might have heard it somewhere," Isabel said. "And forgotten about it, but the subconscious never forgets."

"No, I'm sure that's not what it means. If I had the right interpretation, it would strike a chord in me. I'd know it."

Oliver served a simple green salad, with small round tomatoes and cruets of olive oil and balsamic vinegar.

"Maybe it refers to the murder itself," Lila suggested. "The way it was committed. Dreams are symbolic. Desert stands for dry; irrigation for a liquid. Kruger was limping; had to use a cane. If the carpet, which was as dry as the desert, was wet with oil, he could have slipped, or would have been easier to push down the stairs."

"Not a chance, Mrs. Quinn," Percival said. "The whole area was checked and vacuumed by the technical boys. There was no foreign material there at all, except for a little dust. Very little, at that. You do a good job, Oliver."

"Actually, sir, we have a professional cleaning service. They were in on Tuesday, in preparation for our guests. And now we have an unusual dessert. Fresh sabras."

"We're going to eat Israelis?" Lila quipped.

"The name, sabra, was given to native-born Israelis," Oliver explained, "because of their resemblance to the fruit of the local cactus; tough and prickly on the outside, soft and sweet on the inside. Sabras are sold and eaten outdoors all over Israel all year round. Ping has prepared them by pouring a little Sabra Liqueur over them, a most unusual combination. I hope you like it."

"This is delicious," Lila said. "Were those also Israeli tomatoes in the salad?"

"They are the only tomatoes available at this season which have any flavor. They are quite expensive, but well worth it. Ping has a great dislike for tasteless produce."

"Israel is now selling all sorts of fruits and vegetables all over the world," Lila said. "Flowers, too. I've read about it. They've developed new ways of growing things hydroponically. And new irrigation methods that conserve water. They install perforated pipes under the ground, so every drop of water goes right into the roots and—"

"Not pipes, Lila," Giles shouted. "Hoses! Of course, that's it. *You're* the one who told me, Oliver. Thanks." He got up from the table quickly. "I have to think. I have to rest. I have to plan how ... I'm going to my room. Don't bother me. No one. Oliver, call me at five to ten, in case I fall asleep." He walked quickly to the door of the study.

"May I suggest, sir," Oliver said, "that you take your cane with you?"

"My cane? *You*, Oliver? My *cane*?"

"Yes, sir. Under the circumstances, it might be advisable."

Giles grinned happily and dashed out. In a second, he stuck his head back in again. "I don't want anybody to follow me tonight, or watch me, is that clear? This is a very delicate matter; very touch and go. I don't have the leeway to worry about an additional factor or to scare anyone off. If I can make it work at all." He closed the door.

"Since when has he been like this, Oliver?" Percival asked.

"Quite all right, sir. Mr. Giles has just figured out who the murderer is and is planning the campaign to apprehend him."

"Just catch? The DA wants proof, Oliver."

"Mr. Giles is an attorney, sir, and I am sure he understands that need very well. If there is a way to obtain concrete evidence, or a confession, Mr. Giles will produce what is required."

"You sound like you don't think he can, Oliver."

"I'm afraid, sir, in this case, as I see it, it is not possible. However, I am not privy to what Mr. Giles has in mind."

"But he said you told him."

"I have told Mr. Giles many things in the past few days, sir. At present, I see no connection with anything I might have said in the discussion prior to his achieving understanding of the problem."

"We were talking, that is, Mrs. Quinn was talking, about Israeli vegetables and irrigation methods, just before he jumped."

"Yes sir, but Mr. Giles has a very methodical way of thinking, which is sometimes not overly rapid. He may have suddenly realized how something I had said earlier fitted into what Mrs. Quinn had said, and the synergy produced the solution."

"Well, will you at least think about what you said to him since the murder?"

"Yes, sir. I have been searching my memory as we have been talking, and I believe that I now understand what Mr. Giles had in mind."

"You do, Oliver?" Isabel was wide-eyed. "Tell me, quickly, before I explode."

"I regret, madam, that I cannot. Mr. Giles does not want anyone to interfere in this operation, and in this he is quite right. It could prove harmful."

"I won't interfere, Oliver; I just want to know."

"I am thankful, madam, that in a recent event, your independence of mind was quite helpful, but in this case, I'm afraid, your impulsiveness might prove dangerous. You can help in one way, however."

"I think I have just been insulted in a very complimentary way, Oliver, but we'll discuss that later. How can I help?"

"I require four pairs of your pantyhose, madam, which I may not return whole. I will obtain others for you tomorrow."

"Four pairs? I left in a big hurry and I only took three, and I'm wearing one pair now."

"I can spare two pairs," Lila said. "Or do they have to be Isabel's? Mine are not sheer; hides the varicose veins. Does color matter?"

"Not at all, madam. I'll send the floor maid to each of your rooms."

"But Giles does not want anyone to disturb him," Isabel said. "Not even me."

"Gina will not disturb him, madam, as you would, and she knows where everything is. One more thing, Mr. Percival. Would you please stay here in the study with Miss Isabel and Mrs. Quinn until ten after ten?"

"To keep them from sneaking out?"

"Not at all, sir. Their good judgment, as well as their ignorance of Mr. Giles's plan, is sufficient warranty of their proper behavior. I must prepare something in your room, sir, that is all."

"You realize, Oliver, that I'm not going to do what Giles said. There's no way I'm going to let him mess with a killer and me not knowing what's going on."

"I quite understand, sir. Then let me suggest, sir, that at five to ten you go quietly to your room and put the chain on your door. Open it a crack and observe. If you are needed, you can be in the thick of things in a second."

"Can I do the same?" Isabel asked.

"I don't believe that will cause any harm. But please, keep your room lights out, your drapes drawn, and don't make a sound, no matter what you see or hear."

"Okay, but don't join, the orgy?" Isabel said sarcastically.

"Precisely, madam. For Mr. Giles's sake."

43

At ten to ten, Percival Sullivan turned out all
the lights in his room, tilted the venetians as tightly as he
could get them, and pulled the drapes closed. He adjusted
the drapes so that no light from the street penetrated the
darkness. He loosened the .38 Police Special he always carried in its back-belt holster and walked softly to the door of
the bedroom. Slowly and quietly he eased open the door an
inch, put his eye to the crack, and waited.

At six minutes to ten, Lila Quinn opened the door of her
bedroom two inches, slipped a spring hair curler into the
gap, and piled three books on the floor against the door to
hold it in its slightly opened position. She pulled a footstool
over, sat down and leaned forward, cheekbone pressed against
the doorjamb, looking down the second-floor corridor along
the stair partition toward the door to Giles Sullivan's bedroom, and waited.

At exactly three minutes to ten, Giles Sullivan picked up
his gold-headed cane, twisted it open with a practiced hand,
pulled the saber swiftly and smoothly out of its wooden
scabbard, and loosened up with a few fast cuts and thrusts
in the middle of the bedroom. He snapped the saber back
into its scabbard and twisted the haft to a tight lock. He
moved forward toward the door, gracefully, now with an
athlete's balance and alertness, and, still holding the sword
cane in his left hand, put both arms around the waiting Isabel
Macintosh. They held each other closely, silently, for several
seconds, not moving, not kissing. Isabel let go first, stepping
back and opening the door for Giles. He strode into the dimly
lit hall, moving slowly and purposefully. As he started up

the stairs, Isabel moved into the open doorway and stood there, hands hanging limply at her sides, waiting.

Lila watched Giles leave his room and enter the stairwell. She watched Isabel standing in the doorway. Lila hesitated, then slipped off her shoes. She opened her door slowly and walked silently toward Isabel. As she passed the stairwell, she glanced upward; Giles was already out of sight. Lila went to Isabel and held her tightly for a moment. She took Isabel's right hand in her left hand and took up a position beside her in the open doorway, waiting.

At one minute to ten, Percival saw Giles come off the third-floor landing, walk past Gloria Raffa's door and the corridor to Sondra Stempel's room, directly toward Percival's bedroom. At the stair landing, Giles turned right, up to the fourth floor. Percival took out his revolver, snapped off the safety, and opened his door six inches. He heard a faint knock from upstairs, and leaned against the wall, waiting.

At ten thirty-one, the door opened, spilling a bright rectangle of light on the floor of the dark hallway, and Giles Sullivan left Victoria van Broek's bedroom. He moved very slowly, directly forward, to the head of the stairs leading down to the third floor. Jauntily, he tipped his gold-headed cane over his right shoulder, angled it across the back of his head, and stood on the stair landing, looking down.

As soon as he reached the landing, Victoria van Broek followed silently, in stockinged feet. The waist of the doubled pantyhose was wound around her arthritic right hand, its sand-loaded toe swinging behind. As she approached Giles, she drew her arm back to deliver the stunning blow to his head, then changed the angle of her swing to the vertical, to avoid the protective cane. At that instant, from the end of the dark cross-corridor, the *bolas* Oliver had thrown, made of two doubled pairs of pantyhose sewn together at their waists, their toes loaded with earth, whirled around Victoria van Broek, wrapping themselves around her body and uplifted arm like a straightjacket. Her forward momentum carried her to the stair, slipping past Giles, teetering for a moment before she went down, head first. She screamed once, before she hit the third-floor landing.

Percival bounded out of his room the moment he heard the scream. He was at the stair landing the moment Victoria's head hit the floor. Percival straddled the limp woman with his knees and leaned over, his broad torso completely shielding the tiny body from Giles's view, the motion of his thick shoulders unreadable. When Giles reached the bottom of the stair, Percival was gently unwinding the makeshift cosh from Victoria van Broek's unresisting right hand. He then started unwinding the *bolas* from her body, moving his huge hands carefully so as not to disturb her clothes or the position of her body. "I'll call Faber after we talk," he said quietly to Giles.

"How is she?" Giles asked.

"Broken neck," Percival said. "She was dead when I got there."

44

"**I** TOLD THE OTHER FOUR THAT THERE HAD BEEN AN ACCI-dent," Oliver said, "and to stay in their rooms until the police were done with them. Carmen and Agnes are in position on their respective floors. All is secure."

"Why didn't they all come running out," Isabel asked, "when Victoria screamed?"

"The day after Kruger was murdered?" Lila asked. "Are you kidding? If I were one of them and heard a scream in the night, I wouldn't unbolt my door for anything."

"What was that thing you threw, Oliver," Percival asked, "that wrapped around her like an octopus?"

"*Bolas*," Oliver said. "The Argentinian *gauchos* don't use lassos as your American cowboys do; they use *bolas*, a cord with a round ball of stone on each end. In the middle of that cord another cord is tied. This cord has a slightly smaller ball at its end. Whirl the weights around your head and let go. When the *bolas* are released, they fly out into a whirling wheel. When that hits a steer, the weights wrap the cords tightly around the animal's legs, causing it to fall to the ground. Much more efficient than a lasso, where the steer can drag a cowboy out of his saddle, if he's careless."

"What I took off her had four weights."

"Yes, sir," Oliver said. "Pantyhose come with two legs each. I sewed the middles of two pairs of pantyhose together with the legs outstanding to make the equivalent of a four-armed *bolas*."

"Then why did you need four pairs?" Lila asked.

"I had considered the possibility," Oliver said blandly, "that an accident to Miss Victoria might occur, and that the police would have to be called. I did not want them to find any grains of sand or earth in the carpet, and it would look very suspicious if I vacuumed the carpet just before the police arrived. I, therefore, had to double the pantyhose by putting one set inside another, to make sure that nothing could get through the material. It was useful, madam, that your pantyhose, as is so often the case with mature ladies, were not sheer."

"But why didn't we find any sand or dirt when she hit Kruger on the head?" Percival asked. "Her cosh had only a single leg."

"No, sir, it was a full pair of pantyhose, with the one leg fitted inside the other."

"That can't be," Isabel said. "The feet wouldn't fit. They'd be in opposite directions."

"It can be done, madam. If you will visualize this: hold a pair of pantyhose in normal position in front of you, as if you were ready to put them on. Put your left hand all the way inside the left leg and pull it completely out. Put your left hand, again, inside the now-everted left leg and push it into the right leg. It will fit perfectly, toes in the right direction. If you put some sand in the toe, or, as I did, earth . . ."

"That's why you wanted me out of Kruger's room," Percival said. "You wanted to take dirt from my rubber plants."

"Actually, sir, I got the idea from Miss Victoria van Broek. When Carmen told me that Miss Victoria had washed a pair of pantyhose and watered the cacti on Saturday morning, right after Mr. Kruger had fallen downstairs, I thought nothing of it, until Mr. Giles realized the import of the irrigation of the desert and that pipes are hoses. Pantyhoses and cacti. I believe it was I who spoke to him in his dream, since it was I who told him about Carmen's complaint about Miss Victoria in waking life. Dreams tend to refer to reality symbolically, though they are usually more abstruse and difficult to interpret than this one was."

"Where are my pantyhose now?" Lila asked.

"Ping—he's the only one I can really trust—has emptied the earth back in to the rubber plants and the sand from Miss Victoria's cosh into the cacti, and watered those plants sufficiently so as to conceal that any earth had ever been removed. Your articles have been washed and are presently being dried. By the time the police get here, everything will be back in its proper place. Tomorrow, after you are provided with new pantyhose, we will dispose of these."

"You should have saved the cosh for evidence," Percival

said. "Now we have no proof that Victoria killed Kruger; not evidence at all."

"The cosh that struck Kruger no longer exists," Giles said. "Victoria washed it out, remember? Since Victoria is dead, she's not going to fight the case. The cosh that *didn't* strike me is not a murder weapon. If we had saved that, we might have had to explain Oliver's *bolas* and that might have led to his indictment for murder. If we leave Oliver out of it, I might be accused of pushing Victoria down the stairs. No, I think Oliver acted properly to protect us all. We can explain how Victoria killed Kruger and you, Percival, must persuade Faber to accept that. It shouldn't be too hard, since it really happened that way and no other explanation makes sense."

"How do I explain Victoria's death to Faber?"

"An accident. She was old and her conscience troubled her so that she was not careful of her own safety. Surely *one* accident is permissible, since we can explain the murder of Kruger. Is he going to worry about the accidental death of a murderer, especially a dead one?"

Percival wrinkled his brow in thought for a minute, then brightened. "He'll buy it," Percival decided. "You did solve the Kruger murder for him."

"It still doesn't fit," Lila said. "Even after she hit Kruger, knocked him out, there was no guarantee that he would be killed by the fall. We discussed before, that she would have to break Kruger's neck herself to make sure he was dead. With her arthritic hands? Impossible. It was pure luck that *her* neck was broken, but she did have her hands tied up."

"Yes, it was indeed lucky," Oliver said, carefully not looking at Percival. "And it is true that Miss Victoria could not depend on the fall to break Kruger's neck, but she had planned for that, too. She had the waist of the pantyhose cosh wrapped around her right hand and a large lump in the toe of the cosh. All she had to do was turn Kruger's head sideways and grasp the lump of the cosh in her left hand. Slip the loop of pantyhose around Mr. Kruger's head, put her stockinged foot between his shoulderblades, and lean back fast. That will produce a broken neck every time."

"Are you sure, Oliver?" Percival asked.

"According to my whodunits," Oliver said, "it is the preferred method when one is small and weak. Leaves no marks and no fingerprints."

"You timed your throw perfectly," Percival said. "Giles was very lucky. A second later..."

"My greatest concern was when Mr. Giles walked out of Miss Victoria's room. Even though he was trying to walk slowly, he did not move as slowly as Mr. Kruger must have, handicapped as he was with excess weight, a bad hip and a cane. Fortunately, Mr. Giles thought to halt at the head of the stairs, giving Miss Victoria time to reach him before he started down."

"But why did she kill Kruger in the first place?" Percival asked. "Why take the risk?"

"It is pretty certain," Giles responded, "that Kruger had the idea that the key to the message lay in the directions in the will rather than in the crosswords, but he couldn't go any further. When he called Victoria and told her that, in return for giving her the way to find the message she must sign a will in his favor, she understood she would have a very short time to live after she inherited. She knew she would have to kill Kruger to save her own life as well as to get the handwritten will back. So she did what Kruger had, essentially, forced her to do."

"I don't understand why there was no bump on Kruger's head," Lila said. "We turned down the idea that he was hit because it would show."

"We assumed Kruger being hit in the killer's room and his body thrown down the stairs later. During that time, a bump would have had time to rise on his head. It would have been immediately visible, since his head was shaved. This way, Kruger was dead seconds after he was hit. All circulation stopped and the body fluids, in fact, would have collected at his face, away from the back of his head."

"Victoria certainly had me fooled," Isabel said. "Who'd have thought...?"

"One should never underestimate senior citizens," Oliver said. "We five are excellent examples of that. And Miss Victoria, of course, was truly skilled in both planning and execution."

"You mean she planned Kruger's murder when she came here on Wednesday?" Isabel said skeptically. "I don't believe it. How could she have known?"

"She did not plan anything then, madam, but she did, very rapidly, take advantage of the existing situation and improvised the means to carry out her plans."

"She was a true daughter of her father," Lila said. "If it hadn't ended that way, and if no one had gotten the secret message, I probably would have recommended her for the inheritance. What a brain, to have figured out this whole scheme in the time she had from when Kruger called her to when she killed him."

"I think you will find, madam, that Miss Victoria was not totally inexperienced in having her way, by one means or another."

"Victoria van Broek started her career of murder long ago." Giles finally spoke. "Before she was a senior citizen. She killed her husband."

"How do you know?" Percival asked intently. "You sure?"

"Absolutely sure, Percival. No proof, of course, but look at the facts. She wanted large cacti in her room, plants with dry sandy soil. Was she planning to kill anyone when she arrived? Not necessarily, but it was, for her, just an ordinary business precaution. Is it possible that she thought the whole thing out at that moment? As well as insisting on the room at the head of the upper-floor stairs? Not very likely. No, she had done something like this before. To her husband. With silk stockings. He had been drinking the night he died, but he was not drunk. The balcony railing was almost four feet high. That's up to here." Giles put his hand at the bottom of his breastbone. "They had run out of money. His insurance was the only asset they had left, the policy that Victoria has been living off, barely, for the last half of her life. One bash at the back of his head while he was standing at the balcony railing, lift his feet, and bango, Victoria was a widow. Everyone suspected suicide, but the van Broek family, particularly Victoria's mother, hushed it up. Under those conditions, who would dare to accuse Victoria van Broek of murder? And how could you prove it, if you did?"

"She was a multiple murderer?" Percival stared at Giles. "That's good, Giles; that's very good. I'm going to let Faber open up that case, if you don't mind. He's a good guy and I'd like to do him a favor."

"You want him owing you, Percival?"

"That's the way the world works, Giles."

"Then here's another for you, Perce. Victoria killed her father, too."

"He died of a heart attack, Giles. Absolutely. Faber and I checked everybody out, all the way back to year one."

"Oh, yes, he did die of a heart attack, Percival, but Victoria killed him. She told us how she and the other Broek children used to go up to the fourth floor and drop tennis balls down the big square stairwell, right in front of the servant's noses. Scared them *half* to death, she said. Well, she did that to her father, too. It was right after he had eaten a very heavy meal. He had suffered one heart attack recently, and she scared him *all the way* to death."

"With a tennis ball, Giles? I don't believe it."

"Not with a tennis ball, Percival; with a big Delft vase. The one that was found on the floor, broken, next to his body. The one that they thought he swept off its pedestal when he had the attack."

"No way, Giles. She could never bomb him that accurately from four floors up. And the type of break and the size of the particles showed that it only fell a few feet. The cover, in fact, was lying on top of his legs, unbroken."

"It did only fall a few feet. She had taken it up to the second floor and was leaning over the balustrade, holding the vase with one hand inside its neck. From that short distance she could drop it quite accurately. She dropped the cover on his legs after he fell over. Can you imagine the effect on a man who had just overeaten heavily, a fat, middle-aged man with a recently injured heart, to have a big expensive vase whiz past his nose and explode at his feet? It's a wonder he wasn't dead *before* the doctor got there."

"But why, Giles?" Isabel asked. "She loved her father, from the way she talked about him."

"She loved her *Daddy*, her Sugar Daddy, Isabel. She loved luxury, Isabel, money and what it could buy. And she always had to have her own way. She killed her father because he wouldn't let her marry Carl Locherwald and, I'm sure, Carl wouldn't have married her without a big dowry. In those days, the father's consent was still important, especially in first-generation traditional families and especially when Daddy controlled the purse strings. So she inherited the money and they were married only six months after her father's death."

"That sounds right, too, Giles." Percival sounded pleased. "Mind if I give this to Faber, too?"

"Not at all, Perce. You really want to get a lot of hooks into Faber, don't you?"

"Damn right I do. I want to get this case closed fast, without too many questions. You know how it looks to have two deaths in exactly the same way in exactly the same place in five days? Even a kid right out of the police academy would get suspicious. This has got to be a *very* short investigation if I can help it."

"What were you doing while I was coming down the stairs?"

"Checking to see if her neck was broken. It was."

"I suggest, sir," Oliver said hurriedly, "that you follow Mr. Percival's advice. The sooner we get back to normal, the better. There will be enough problems with the estate as it is."

"No there won't," Giles said confidently. "I have that all figured out. Victoria found the hidden message; that was evident when she let me in at the first soft knock."

"True, sir. She had no objection to letting you in and signing anything you wished, since she intended to take the papers off your body after she killed you, just as she had done with Mr. Kruger. I took the liberty of searching Miss Victoria's room right after the accident and found the secret message, in the clear, on her desk. The original is now in the safe here in the study, with her fingerprints still on it. I can return it if you wish."

"No, it's perfect where it is; she could have shown it to me on Saturday morning, and I'm going to claim that's what was done. With the cooperation of Lila and Isabel."

"You're going to *lie*, Giles?" Isabel asked.

"In the service of a higher morality. It's not much of a lie; she did have the solution by Saturday morning."

"And you weren't going to announce it," Lila said, "until the bank officer agreed it was the correct solution, when the bank opened Monday morning. Which is why we had to continue the extra crosswords, in case Victoria's solution was incorrect."

"Exactly."

"The other four won't like it," Isabel said.

"They have no choice, Isabel; the will is quite clear on this. Kruger couldn't inherit because he didn't find the hidden message. Vicki found the hidden message; she *must* inherit and the others must get nothing. But Victoria can't inherit either. Not only is the criminal not permitted to benefit from his crime, but in equity, which controls estates and inheritance, an heir cannot inherit if he kills an ancestor in order to inherit, nor can he kill a rival heir for the same purpose. Had not Victoria killed Kruger, he might very well have found the secret message before she did. The other four, Gloria, Sondra, Eileen, and Richard, were out of the picture the moment Victoria found the hidden message."

"But shouldn't Victoria have been disqualified for collusion with Kruger, since it happened before she found the secret message?" Lila was troubled. "And doesn't that throw everything open again?"

"We have no evidence that they met for purposes of collusion, much less that they actually colluded. There could be many reasons why they met, so we cannot disqualify Victoria. In fact, we have no evidence that Kruger went into her room, or even spoke to her. They might have met in the hall, and she pushed him down the stairs as he passed her. Further, we don't know when she solved the puzzle and found the hidden message. If she found it early Friday night, what she did afterward has no bearing on whether or not she inherited, even if she colluded. Even if she found it five minutes before she—had the accident, she is still the only possible heir. The other four, Gloria, Sondra, Richard, and Eileen, were *completely* out of the picture, the moment Victoria found the message. However, as a result of her actions, Victoria cannot inherit, nor can her estate."

"So the State gets all the money?" Isabel asked. "That's not fair."

"No. In such circumstances, the money goes to the contingent remainderman. In this case, the Boy Scouts of America, a truly worthy organization."

"So each loose end is tied up very satisfactorily in neat little bows," Lila said, contentedly.

"*Bolas*," Isabel said. "Neat little bows and cute little *bolas*. Big *bolas*, for which let us thank God and Eros. And thanks to the *bolas*, I can have what's left of a proper vacation. It's late, now; I'm going to bed. Coming, Giles?"

Puzzle No. 1

Puzzle No. 2

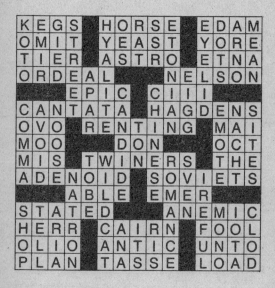

K	E	G	S		H	O	R	S	E		E	D	A	M
O	M	I	T		Y	E	A	S	T		Y	O	R	E
T	I	E	R		A	S	T	R	O		E	T	N	A
O	R	D	E	A	L			N	E	L	S	O	N	
		E	P	I	C		C	I	I	I				
C	A	N	T	A	T	A		H	A	G	D	E	N	S
O	V	O		R	E	N	T	I	N	G		M	A	I
M	O	O			D	O	N				O	C	T	
M	I	S		T	W	I	N	E	R	S		T	H	E
A	D	E	N	O	I	D		S	O	V	I	E	T	S
		A	B	L	E		E	M	E	R				
S	T	A	T	E	D			A	N	E	M	I	C	
H	E	R	R		C	A	I	R	N		F	O	O	L
O	L	I	O		A	N	T	I	C		U	N	T	O
P	L	A	N		T	A	S	S	E		L	O	A	D

Puzzle No. 3

Puzzle No. 4

```
I S M E   P A I D       S I M P
O P E N   A L L I S     T O M E
W A N T   T E E T H   Y O D A
A S S O R T E D   O C L O C K
      M O E       R O I
  U M B E R   T W E E Z E R S
W R Y   N E R O     E V E N
E G G S   S L A N T   S I L O
P E U T   K I T H     L I B
T R Y I N G O N   I M U S T
      M O R       R O N
T R A U M A   L A T C H K E Y
R O L L   C R A K E   U N D O
A B O U   E A D I E   S E E S
P E G S   H Y M N   K E N T
```

Puzzle No. 5

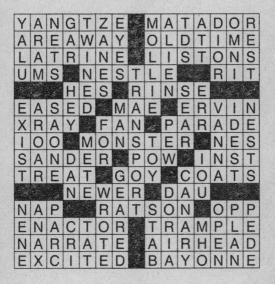

YANGTZE MATADOR
AREAWAY OLDTIME
LATRINE LISTONS
UMS NESTLE RIT
HES RINSE
EASED MAE ERVIN
XRAY FAN PARADE
IOO MONSTER NES
SANDER POW INST
TREAT GOY COATS
NEWER DAU
NAP RATSON OPP
ENACTOR TRAMPLE
NARRATE AIRHEAD
EXCITED BAYONNE

Attention Mystery and Suspense Fans

Do you want to complete your collection of mystery and suspense stories by some of your favorite authors? John D. MacDonald, Helen MacInnes, Dick Francis, Amanda Cross, Ruth Rendell, Alistar MacLean, Erle Stanley Gardner, Cornell Woolrich, among many others, are included in Ballantine/Fawcett's new Mystery Brochure.

For your FREE Mystery Brochure, fill in the coupon below and mail it to: